Entangled Mafia Princess

Em Brown

D1332878

Wind Color Press

Contents

Chapter 1

Kai

"**B**AD DAY?" RAFE LEE guesses as soon as I soon as I walk into the study of my home in Marin County overlooking the bay and Golden Gate Bridge.

"A shit day," I acknowledge.

Rafe shows me the glass he holds. "I helped myself to a drink."

I nod before sitting down opposite him. Rafe and I belong to the same triad, but we connected because we were both raised by our grandmothers. Rafe lost his parents to suicide and murder. Mine were killed in an automobile accident. When our grandmothers passed away, the Jing San Triad became our new family.

"You here on business?" I ask him.

"Passing through. I'm headed to Europe. But what happened with you?"

To calm myself, I draw in long breaths as I listen to the crackle of the fire in the fireplace. Back when I lived in Heihe, China, a city on the border with Russia, where winter temperatures easily dropped below zero, the warmth of a fire was something to be savored. In the San Francisco Bay Area, where winter temperatures can soar into the seventies, fireplaces often seem more decorative than anything else.

"I had an unexpected setback," I reply.

My latest endeavor was supposed to catapult me up the ranks of the Jing San Triad and make me a legend within the organization. But what was supposed to have been the *pièce de résistance* of my career slipped from me. The amount of money I could have secured from the sale of the artificial intelligence I had stolen from SVATR, Silicon Valley Advanced Technologies and Robotics, would have eclipsed all my previous arms trades combined.

It was bad enough that my prized take was stolen from me, but the salt into the wound was how long and hard Michael's wife had sobbed when I had to break the news to her that her husband had been killed in the effort. It wasn't the first time I'd had to inform a woman she was now a widow, but it didn't get any easier. The women always remind me of how my grandmother cried when my grandfather passed away. I was just a small kid at the time, but I remember it more than I remember the deaths of my parents a few years before.

"Anything I can help with?" Rafe asks.

It had taken months and months of planning and thousands of dollars in bribery before we could break into the heavily fortified offices, hack into the SVATR server, and download the encrypted information onto a laptop equipped with SVATR security clearance. I'm not about to have all that effort go to waste.

Not wanting to trouble Rafe just before his trip, however, I reply, "It's okay. I just need to regroup."

Rafe only looks at me with those dark, intense eyes of his. He can probably see the truth, but he respects my boundaries enough not to question me. Normally I wouldn't hesitate to confide in him. Rafe is like the older brother I never had. Though he doesn't divulge much, I sense he has his demons, but he always appears suave and collected. His personality is the opposite of my friend Andrian Plotnikov, whom I partnered with on the SVATR heist. Rafe's cautioned me about Andrian, and I know he wouldn't approve of my working with Andrian on such a significant endeavor.

"You let me know if you need anything," Rafe says before we turn to more banal subject matters.

After he departs, I text my right-hand man, Andy Huang, for an update. Even though Andy was injured in the ambush shortly after leaving SVATR, our guys were able to down one of the attackers before they made off with our laptop.

Who did this? And who could have betrayed our plans? I rub my temple.

Athena, a German Shepherd I rescued from the Tenderloin District when she was barely a year old, paddles into the room. As if she knows I could use comforting, she rests her head upon my lap and licks at my hand when I stroke her head.

Andy calls me back. "We got a name."

I sit up. "Yeah?"

"He works for Liam Callaghan."

"Liam Callaghan. Who the fuck is that?"

"Don't know. I can continue with the waterboarding. Or we can switch things up and start pulling teeth."

Noticing an incoming call from a blocked number, I say, "I'll call you back."

Without picking up the other call, I know it's Andrian. We've known each other since we were boys growing up in the conurbation of Heihe and Blagoveshchensk.

"Dmitri didn't make it," Andrian informs me after I pick up the call. "He died from his gunshot wounds."

"Shit, I'm sorry," I reply in Russian, a language many residents in Heihe learned to welcome their neighbors from across the border. Dmitri, Andrian's most trusted lieutenant, is a significant loss and a personal one.

Andrian pounds what sounds like a table and curses. "How are your guys?"

"I lost Michael," I answer, "and Andy was hit in the shoulder, but he's okay."

"*Yebat'!* You get anything out of the *ubl'udak* that was caught?"

"Liam Callaghan."

"Liam who?"

"Callaghan. Sounds Irish."

"You wait. I make quick call to Belinsky and ask about this Callaghan."

Belinksy is part of the Russian mafia in New York. The Jing San has people on the East Coast, too, and I make a mental list of who I can reach out to.

A few minutes later, Andrian calls again. "Callaghan. From Boston. Belinksy, he thinks the Irish are looking to expand west."

I know the Irish mafia has a presence in places like Chicago, St. Louis, and Omaha, but I've yet to encounter them as far west as California.

"Why the fuck they have to come out here?" Andrian asks.

"Maybe the same reason you came out from Saint Petersburg, Florida."

"I want to give this Callaghan a new asshole. I pulled all my hackers to work on this project. *Chert voz'mi!* And the timing is terrible. The boss wants me in Moscow tomorrow. Says it's important."

"Then you should go. I'll take care of this."

"I'm going to blow this fucking Liam Callaghan to pieces first."

"That won't get us the laptop back."

Andrian pounds the table again and unleashes a string of curses. I let my friend vent—Andrian always was a hothead—but eventually interrupt the tirade, saying, "Andrian, focus. Our guys got ambushed. By a punk. Chances are we've got a traitor, among your people or mine, or both."

At that, Andrian calms enough to say, "Fuck. When I find out who it is, I'm going to tear the bastard's testicles out and shove it down his throat."

"Do that. We need to find the leak as soon as possible and make an example of him."

"You'll check your people, too?"

"Of course."

"I'll talk more with my people back on the East Coast, see what they know about this Liam Callaghan."

"Good. Give my regards to Lukashenko."

"*Do svidaniya.*"

After hanging up, I call back Andy. "Get what you can out of the guy, then dig into this Liam Callaghan."

As I sit with Athena napping at my feet, I mentally comb through all the people who might have tipped Callaghan off to our plans. Aside from a few of my guys, I haven't told anyone in the triad of my effort to acquire the artificial intelligence from SVATR or that I was partnering with my childhood friend in the Russian mafia to pull it off. So there's only a handful of people who could be the problem.

Needing to vent my emotions, I head down to my personal gym. Andrian likes to break things when he's frustrated, but I prefer to pound weights. I'm sculpted but not overly beefy. Too much muscle and the wrong workout can diminish dexterity and quickness, two qualities that got me through my years living on the streets of Heihe before it became a prosperous city with tree-lined boulevards and luxury hotels.

I was a late bloomer and a scrawny boy in my early teen years. There were plenty of times when, after getting beat up by Russian teenagers in Blagoveshchensk, I wished I had been bigger and stronger. Now that I am, I could easily take on the jerks who stole the cheap Chinese goods I tried to sell or who kicked me while I was down because they resented those from Heihe as the city became visibly more and more prosperous compared to Blagoveshchensk. A part of me would relish the opportunity to confront my boyhood tormentors today. Or it might be as fulfilling, certainly easier, to have my bodyguard put a 0.45 between their eyes. But the better part of me is content to leave my past behind me.

"This is what I have so far on Liam Callaghan," Andy tells me after I've finished my workout, showered, and sat down for dinner. "Couldn't get much more out of the guy we've got. He kept passing out."

I glance through the dossier Andy handed me, taking in Liam's background, how he worked his way up the mob in Boston, where he lives, what properties he owns, and, last but not least, his family. The man is married with one son, currently in Ireland, and a daughter who's just about to celebrate her twenty-first birthday.

Chapter 2

Casey

"YOU LOOK LIKE A princess," my aunt, Chloe, coos as the hairdresser places the tiara on my head.

"Or a Barbie doll," says my cousin Hannah, who turned twenty-one a few months before me.

I look at myself in the full-length mirror of a dressing room in the luxury hotel where my birthday party is being held. With my wavy blond hair and bright blue eyes, I bear some resemblance to the dolls I used to play with, but I reply, "I don't have tits big enough to look like Barbie."

"They've made the doll a lot more realistic these days."

Chloe adjusts the tie of my halter dress. "Either way, Kenton Brady is going to eat you up when he sees you."

"Totally," agrees Hannah.

I try to hide a roll of the eyes, but my mother, sitting across from me on the sofa with a martini in hand, catches it anyway. Grace Callaghan, a picture of elegance, has enough natural beauty that one would not guess that she has undergone several Botox injections and collagen treatments. Her low-cut sparkling black dress shows off her breasts, which she had enlarged when she was a teenager.

"What's that look for?" my mother asks.

"I'm not looking to impress Kenton," I answer.

Grace sighs. "It's time you dated nice Irish boys."

"I don't know any nice Irish boys. Do you?"

My mother narrows her eyes at me, which I ignore. We both know that my father is hardly a "good Irish boy" unless "good" means being a successful member of the Mafia and a husband who cheats on his wife with women barely older than his daughter.

And Kenton's hardly a shining example of goodness either. He was a senior at Notre Dame when I was a freshman. He was known for throwing raging parties with his roommates at their off-campus apartment. On two separate occasions, guests had ended up in the hospital from overdrinking.

"Kenton cut short his vacation in Bali just to attend your birthday party, and his father is flying out from St. Louis."

"I didn't ask him to do that."

"No, your father did. Mr. Brady will be here too."

The Brady family head a Mafia in Missouri. This party isn't so much a birthday celebration as it is a networking event for my father.

"Let's just get this over with," I grumble. I'd rather spend my winter break at Mammoth Mountain, where I had picked up snowboarding shortly after we had moved to California. I love the sport, but my mother isn't keen on me getting injured. *At least stick to skiing, which has some sophistication,* my mother had said.

"My dear, you look beautiful," my father greets me when I meet him downstairs in the ballroom. "I can't believe you're twenty-one now."

Nearing fifty, my father has a dusting of gray above the ears. Though his eyes are set a little close together, he's otherwise a handsome man and looks sharp in his white sports coat over a black silk shirt.

"Mr. Brady said he and his son will try to be the first guests to arrive," my father tells me while the other women walk ahead and check on the long buffet table, "so you might have Kenton all to yourself before the other girls get to him."

"That's okay. I'm not really interested in Kenton," I respond.

My father stops. "Not interested in one of the hottest and most eligible bachelors this side of the Mississippi?"

I almost laugh at hearing my father describe another man as "hottest."

"I don't think he's relationship material," I say, recalling the many girls Kenton had been with at Notre Dame.

"Don't worry, his father will take care of that."

"How?"

"In fact, I believe Mr. Brady has already impressed upon Kenton the advantages of merging the Callaghans with the Bradys."

I frown. "Merging? Are we talking about a company?"

"That and more."

"You and Mr. Brady get along well. What else do you need?"

"If you and Kenton were to get married, it would solidify our collective interests."

"Seriously? Are we living in feudal times all of a sudden?"

"My line of business—our society—is a little different."

My chest tightens. "First of all, I never said I was interested in marrying. I'm only turning twenty-one for chrissake. And if I ever did want to get married, which I doubt, it wouldn't be to Kenton Brady."

A cloud passes over my father's face but he tries to remain calm. "You haven't even given the boy a chance. You overlapped at Notre Dame for only a year."

"I doubt he's changed since graduating."

"He'll settle down once he's married and has kids."

"Like you did?" I ask pointedly.

He purses his lips in displeasure. "Casey, you aren't going to find anyone better than Kenton Brady. He'll take over his father's operations one day, just like your brother will be taking over mine."

"Then you should have Jake marry Kenton. Gay marriage is legal here in California."

Pulling away, I go over to where Hannah stands admiring the three-layered cake decorated in dog roses. I can't believe my father. What he's talking about is an arranged marriage. Did he forget we're living in the 21st century? Who does that?

Well, he can't make me marry Kenton. And I doubt Kenton would really want to marry me either.

"This cake looks so good," Hannah says, "but I'd probably have to go to the gym twice to work off the calories from it."

"Come with me to Tahoe and you can work the cake off on the slopes," I implore. Not only do I want to snowboard, I want to get away.

"You know I don't ski."

"I told you I'd teach you to snowboard. Anytime."

"Thanks, but winter sports aren't really my thing."

"Fine. You don't have to hit the slopes. You can come up for the hot tub or the casinos in Nevada."

"But *you're* going to be on the slopes. What am I going to do in the meantime?"

I sigh. My ideal birthday would be a trip to Mammoth Mountain, but no one in my family is into activities involving snow. I have friends at Notre

Dame who ski, and one of them lives in Colorado, so maybe I'll fly out there instead of going to Tahoe.

"I'll be right back," Hannah tells me. "I think one of my lashes is coming unglued."

While Hannah heads to the restroom, I stare at the cake. My birthday party hasn't even started and already I want to leave. Feeling antisocial, I look around for a place I can have some alone time.

I see a little girl about ten years old sitting by herself on a chair against the far wall. Not recognizing her, I go over. She has a handheld video game device.

"That almost looks like the snowboarder Chloe Kim," I remark of the animated character gliding through the air.

"It is," says the girl.

"No way! Chloe's in a video game?"

I watch as the character lands on the ground, runs up to a chest and opens it to reveal munitions and a medical kit.

"There are a lot of skins to choose from in Fortnite," the girl explains.

"Mind if I watch?"

She looks at me in surprise. "Um, I guess."

I sit down and watch her play. The video game has nothing to do with snowboarding. Instead, it's a battle game in which players attempt to eliminate each other to be the last one standing.

"You seem very good," I say to the girl.

She smiles. "Really? You don't think it's weird that I play Fortnite?"

"Why would I think it's weird?"

"Kids at my school say that Fortnite is a boys' game."

"That's sexist. And what does it matter to them that you like Fortnite? You do you. It looks like a fun game, and that Chloe Kim character—"

"It's called a skin."

"That skin is the bomb."

I watch the girl play some more until my father waves me over. Kenton and his father have arrived.

*****

"That was such a cute slideshow," Hannah tells me as the party winds down. "I loved the pic of you on the training potty. And it was sweet of your brother to call in live from Ireland."

I finish off my second slice of cake, glad I made it through all the small talk with everyone. Now I'm going to gift myself a little something by way of a place called Club de Sade.

But my plans are delayed when Kenton comes up and puts an arm around each of us.

"Ready to start the real celebration, ladies?" he asks.

"The real celebration?" I ask.

"Lucky O'Leary's."

His cousin, Andrew, seconds the idea.

"I don't know if I'm up for it," I reply.

"Not up for what?" my father asks as he approaches.

"Rite of passage, Mr. Callaghan," Kenton explains. "At Lucky O'Leary's."

"I know the place. You kids have fun." He turns to me. "Chase will drive you."

I sigh. Chase is my bodyguard, and though my family has had one most of my life, the older I get, the more I dislike the security detail.

"Just one round of drinks," I say. "I don't know that I'm up for much tonight."

My father raises a brow. "Are you turning twenty-one or eighty-one, Casey?"

If I arrive drunk at Club de Sade, they might not let me in. Even if they did, I prefer not to be under the influence when it comes to BDSM, my drug of choice, and I want the full experience, unadulterated by alcohol.

"Let me just change," I say, reaching for my tiara.

"No!" Hannah protests. "That has to stay on, birthday girl."

I roll my eyes. "Seriously? I'm going to a bar wearing a tiara?"

"That way everyone will know it's your special day."

"Will you think about going to Tahoe with me if I wear it?"

"Fine."

Satisfied, I go with them to the bar. In addition to Hannah, Kenton, and Andrew, we invite Kenton's other cousin, Ciara, Hannah's brother, Conor, and a family friend, Fiona. The more people there are, the less I'll be missed if I want to take off early to go to Club de Sade.

At Lucky O'Leary's, we pull two chairs up to a large booth. Hannah maneuvers it so I end up sitting next to Kenton. We all start off with Guinness, then some of the guys and Ciara move onto hard liquor while Hannah opts for a Fat Frog and Fiona goes for another Guinness.

"You plan on nursing that Guinness the whole night?" Kenton asks me.

"Pretty much."

He shakes his head. "Didn't take you for the prissy kind."

"She's not prissy, she's dainty," Fiona says.

Hannah jumps to my defense. "I've seen Casey do more than a Guinness lots of times."

"So why not on the most momentous birthday of your life?" Andrew asks.

"I'm watching my figure," I lie.

Andrew smirks. "I'll watch it for you."

The guys laugh while I roll my eyes.

Kenton puts his arm around me. "You're gorgeous the way you are, Casey, so live it up. It's your fucking birthday."

The server comes by with more shots of whiskey.

"We should see if they can do like a birthday cake shot," Fiona says.

"What's that?" Hannah asks.

"You mix, like, cake vodka, Bailey's and vanilla frosting. Add some sprinkles along the glass."

"Sounds cute."

"Sounds disgusting," says Kenton. "Cake frosting is the last thing I'd want in a drink."

His hand drops from my shoulder to my thigh. Luckily, I'm sitting at the end of the booth and can get up easily. I motion to Hannah. "Ladies' room."

Hannah, buzzed, stares at me for a few seconds before getting up, too. Once we're in the restroom, I tell her that I'm going to go home.

"Already?" she asks.

"Yeah. Tell the others I'm sick or something," I answer.

She knits her brow. "But Kenton is into you. I think it's pretty obvious."

"I just don't feel it with him," I reply, though I wonder if Kenton buys into the arranged marriage idea? Not wanting to dwell on that topic, however, I say to Hannah, "I'm going out the back door, otherwise, they're going to harass me to stay longer."

"But why? Aren't you having a good time?"

"I don't want Chase to have to hang out by himself much longer," I lie.

"Oh. Sucks you have to cart around a bodyguard."

"Tell me about it. You have fun, though."

After giving her a hug, I head out of the restroom and out a door marked exit. Once outside in the chilly night air, I breathe a sigh of relief. I have a change of clothes in my car. Now my real birthday party can begin.

Chapter 3

Kai

"HEARD THE AMERICAN NAVY seized your shipment to Yemen last fall," says Charlie Lee as he, sitting opposite me, leans back in the lounge chair at The Lotus, an exclusive club catering to members of the Jing San Triad.

I don't like the tone in Charlie's voice, though it's hard to tell the sneer through the Australian accent. Charlie's visiting from Sydney, where he runs narcotics.

"That's old news," I reply as I watch Charlie light a cigarette.

"Still, my condolences on your loss. I heard it included thousands of Chinese Type 56 assault rifles and hundreds of heavy machine guns."

"And sniper rifles," I add nonchalantly.

Charlie exhales a stream of smoke. "Must've been a blow. Lucky it wasn't as bad as the loss that forced your old man into retirement."

I feel a muscle along my jaw tighten. At least he referred to my adoptive father as my old man. Unlike Charlie, I wasn't born a Lee. I got my current name, Lee Kai Fan, from my parents after they adopted me. I had initially tried to rob the couple and probably would have had the shit beat out of me if it hadn't been for my adoptive mother intervening. They had a daughter, but under China's one-child policy at the time, they couldn't try for a son.

"Maybe you should consider moving over to narcotics," Charlie suggests. "You'd make eight, nine figures easy—ten if you're as good as me."

I watch as Charlie looks around for an ashtray. "I'm good. I've got other projects in the works."

"Yeah? Is that why Andrian Plotnikov was here? You're not thinking to partner with him, are you?"

"Why not?"

Charlie frowns as he realizes there's no ashtray in sight.

"Smoking isn't allowed in public places here in San Francisco," I inform him.

"Fuck me dead. The world's going to shit. Can you believe the Kiwis are going smoke-free? Now people want Australia to follow in their footsteps."

"More opportunities for you then."

Charlie is silent as he considers what I said. Reaching for an empty shot glass, he uses it for an ashtray.

"Word is Andrian Plotnikov isn't stable," he says. "And why do you need a Russian anyway?"

"There are benefits to collaboration. It's not new. The triad works with the Camorra in Italy."

Charlie blows out another puff of smoke. "If you're looking to impress the Vanguard, let me give you a piece of advice: don't make decisions based on personal feelings."

"Who said it was personal?"

"You and Andrian go way back, don't you?"

Charlie isn't wrong. After a few thugs in Blagovenshenck jumped me when I was eleven years old, Andrian had approached me with a proposition: I would procure the goods in Heihe and Andrian would help sell them and provide protection on the Russian side. Our partnership lasted several years and we kept in touch even after I moved to California.

"Which is why I can trust him," I reply as I glance at a text that just came in. One of my men has located Casey Callaghan.

"In our line of business, you can't really trust any-one, mate."

I rise to leave. "Thanks for the advice. I've got some for you, too: quit smoking. It's bad for your health."

*****

From my seat in the back of the Escalade, I watch as Casey, wearing a glittery tiara, emerges from the back of the bar and run over to her car, where her bodyguard is napping. When they leave, my driver follows them to the SOMA District, eventually pulling over when they park in front of a warehouse that had yet to be converted into an art gallery, office for the latest high-tech startup, or trendy restaurant.

Well, now this is interesting, I think to myself as I watch her get out of her car and knock on the metal door of the building. There's no signage or any indications that the building is anything but a warehouse, but I know what's on the inside.

"Casey, Casey," I purr, "what would Daddy say if he knew?"

The door opens, and Casey and her bodyguard slip inside. Judging by the confidence with which she approached and entered the building, this is not her first time here. After waiting a minute, I step out of the car and knock on the same metal door.

A man opens the door. "Purpose?"

"Just watching tonight," I reply.

"Price is the same whether you play or not. You have an account with us?"

I take out several hundreds from my wallet. "This should cover it."

The last time I was here, several years ago, the price of admission had been around forty bucks.

The man grunts and allows me passage. After stepping inside, I walk through black curtains to an area illuminated by glowing red lights. A nondescript beat pounds in the background for the patrons as they lounge, writhe, or play. This particular BDSM club specializes in voyeurism. Everything is done out in the open. Several large "stalls" line one side of the building. Tables and chairs spread out along the other side. I've been to this club twice because a woman I had been seeing worked here, but otherwise, I prefer the exclusivity of The Lotus or the vibrancy of The Cross.

I choose the table near the middle. Spotting Casey's bodyguard, I wonder if the guy has ever leaked to Callaghan that his precious princess is into kink. I'm guessing not when the bodyguard begins to flirt with another man. From the research I read on Callaghan, the man has made significant donations to organizations advocating "family values" and against gay marriage. The club might be a secret Casey and her bodyguard share.

A woman wearing a leather mini skirt, fishnet top and lashes so long and thick they are obviously fake, stops at my table. "Hey there, hot stuff. You here alone?"

I take in her attractive curves. Sex would be a nice distraction, but I need to remain focused if I'm going to get my asset back.

"Just watching tonight," I reply.

"I'll check in later—in case you change your mid. Name's Carmen, by the way."

She reaches out a hand encased in fingerless gloves. Not wanting her to return, I ignore her and keep my gaze on the stalls.

"Your loss," Carmen mutters as she walked away. "Asshole."

Unperturbed, I prop my ankle over my knee. A few minutes splayed over my lap and Carmen would soon realize it was *her* loss.

Just then Casey appears. She has on a red satin bustier and matching thong. Five-inch stiletto heels make her slender legs look long. Handcuffs encircle her wrists. A ball gag separates her lips. She has a nice figure, though I like my women fuller in the ass.

Her Dom, wearing black leather pants, walks her to one of the stalls and pushes her down on all fours over a large square ottoman.

"Get that ass higher," the Dom commands.

From my viewpoint, I can't see her backside, which she lifts, though I have an unobstructed view of her face, which is what I prefer at the moment.

The Dom raises the crop he holds and whacks her on the ass. Casey barely flinches. She wiggles her backside, inviting the next spank, which her Dom delivers. The crop falls several times on her buttocks, which are probably a nice shade of pink by now, but I'm unimpressed. The handcuffs Casey wears haven't served much of a purpose so far. If they had been applied behind her back, they would at least cause some discomfort.

The Dom reaches for her breasts and tries to squeeze one through the bustier before unzipping his pants and angling his cock between her thighs.

The guy's done with the foreplay already? I would have had my sub near tears before I considered sinking into her.

Once inside Casey, the Dom starts thrusting away like a teenage boy. She grunts and looks almost bored. In fact, she's scanning the audience as if trying to find something of interest. Her gaze meets mine.

I stare back at her. *That's right, princess, I'm looking at you.*

At first, she looks a little affronted, which she shouldn't be if she's a regular here, then she looks intrigued.

The Dom slaps her ass a few times, but the scene is basically vanilla to me. She keeps my gaze until, with a croak, her Dom comes. After stumbling away, the guy finds a vibrator and holds it to Casey's pussy.

She finds me again.

You wouldn't be so lucky if you were my sub, I say through my gaze. *You'd have to work much harder for me. I'd make you a slobbering mess before I let you come, and you'd love every minute of it.*

As if she understands me, she shivers. I feel myself growing warm in her stare and wonder what her pussy feels like.

Want to know what I can do to you?

I start imagining the answer to my own question. Maybe I'd start by outfitting her in something more constraining. Heat pulses in my groin.

It takes her a little while, but she eventually comes. The Dom removes her handcuffs. Casey undoes the ball gag.

That's it? I shake my head.

"Still just gonna watch?" Carmen asks upon her return.

Casey glances in my direction.

"Maybe," I answer. It's Casey whom I'm interested in, but I allow Carmen to sit at my table.

She gives me a smile with her wide lips. "I didn't catch your name."

"You didn't?" I reply casually, still looking at Casey. "It's 'Asshole.'"

Carmen blushes. "That wasn't meant for you."

"The name suits me."

She blinks, not sure how to react. Instead, she asks, "So, you a top, bottom or switch?"

"Top," I answer. I haven't been a bottom since my early days when I was first learning how to top.

"That top there," I say, looking at Casey's Dom. "He with her?"

"You mean Sean? He's new here. And, no, he's not with Casey."

I watch Casey walk over to her bodyguard. "How do you know?"

"Casey hasn't found a Dom she wants to be regular with, and she's tried just about everyone who's walked in here. I mean, she's a total slut, even by club standards."

"She hasn't tried me."

Carmen leans toward me and flashes her teeth. "That's 'cause I got to you first. Luckily for you."

I notice Casey watching me as Carmen reaches for my thigh. I catch her wrist and hold up her hand in a tight grip, making her gasp.

"I didn't give you permission to touch me," I tell her. "That's a punishable offense."

Chapter 4

Casey

D ELIBERATELY CHOOSING TO WALK by his table, I can hear Carmen. Her eyes widen, then her face softens. "Oh, so you're one of those Doms."

He releases her. "Ready for your punishment?"

She rises eagerly to her feet. "Yes! I mean, yes, Sir."

His voice lowers. "Then let's get started."

I shiver, wishing that sexy baritone was aimed at me. I head into the changing room. My friend Aleisha must have just arrived and is peeling off her wool coat.

"It feels like twenty degrees out there!" she complains.

It's more like fifty-something, but I don't dispute her. "You should try a Boston winter."

"No, thank you. I'd freeze to death."

"Hey, you notice that well-dressed guy with Carmen? He looks new, or at least, I haven't seen him before."

"You mean the guy who looks Asian? Or maybe Wasian? Like Adam Driver."

"I don't think Adam Driver's Wasian."

"He's not? Well, Keanu Reeves, then. I could go for some Wasian. Wait. Blasian. The Rock."

I'm not interested in a Hollywood actor. I'm interested in *him.*

"So you know who he is?" I redirect.

"Never saw him before. I like those broad shoulders. Mmm-yum. Carmen always gets the good ones."

"Lucky bitch," I agree.

"She stole this delicious Dom from me the other night. He was looking at *me* for a long time, but Erika overheard her telling him I had a smelly cunt!"

"Want me to smack her for you? I don't need a reason. It'll just be fun."

"She's got the club owner wrapped around her pinkie. You'd get kicked out."

After I'm dressed, I head out and take a seat next to Chase at his table because it affords me a nice view of the stall where Carmen and the tall, dark, and handsome Dom are playing.

"Strip," I hear the Dom tell Carmen.

She peels off her top. I can't help but stare at her large tits.

"Must be a drag having to cart around those melons all the time," Chase says.

I'm undecided. I like my figure, though there have been times I've wanted a larger bust.

Chase turns his attention to a hunky blond playing with a trans while I watch Carmen step out of her skirt. Now she's in nothing but her thong and five-inch heels.

"Turn around," he orders her.

She does, giving him and everyone else a view of everything. His gaze seems to take it all in, from her brown areolas to her full backside. I wonder if he's an ass man, tits man, or legs man? Carmen has me beat on everything except maybe legs. She only stands about five feet, two inches, so he looks even bigger and taller.

He cradles one of her large tits in his hand, curling each finger independently into her flesh. I lick my bottom lip, wondering what those fingers would feel like on me. Some guys might as well have paws for hands, but this Dom works every digit.

Abruptly, he releases her breast and smacks it, making her yelp in surprise. He backhands the other orb.

"What's your safe word?" he asks.

"*Detener*," she answers.

"*Prefieres español?*"

"*Lo que quiera, Maestro.*"

I wish I knew what they were saying. I half paid attention in French classes at my high school back in Boston.

He grabs her tit again before slapping it.

"You like your tits?" he asks.

"Yes."

"I bet you play with your tits a lot."

She smiles.

"Show me."

She holds her breasts in both hands and pushes them up. She rolls them over her chest and squeezes them before playing with the nipples.

"Kiss them," he tells her.

She gives each orb a smooch.

"Lick them," he says next, "and suck those nipples."

She does as instructed.

"Harder," he commands when the nipple falls quickly from her mouth.

She scoops the bud back between her plump lips. Her boobs might be natural, but her lips have probably seen a syringe or two.

The Dom spanks her. "I said harder."

She pulls the nipple further into her mouth.

"Now bite them."

Carmen hesitates. He lifts a brow, and it's enough to get her to comply.

"Harder," he says again as she nibbles gently on herself.

She hesitates but bites down on her nipple.

"Harder," he repeats.

She drops her nipple. *"Detener."*

I shake my head. Wouldn't have used my safe word that early.

"Let's try something else, then," he says before finding some rope. "Kneel on the bench and put your hands behind your head."

She does as he says, projecting her breasts forward. He wraps the rope around a breast, resulting in a deformed shape that starts to darken in color. I wonder if my breasts are big enough to bind like that.

He slaps the orb now shaped like a tulip bulb. She flinches. He binds her other breast.

When he's done, he tells her to play with herself. "Show me how naughty you get when you're by yourself."

Carmen stuffs a hand into her thong and starts rubbing while he tugs on her nipple.

"Ever been hung by your breasts?" he asks.

Is that possible? I wonder.

Carmen shakes her head.

He angles a breast toward her mouth. "Lick the nipple."

She sticks out her tongue to reach the nub. Her breasts take on a purplish hue.

"Keep that tongue out," he tells her after releasing her breast to adjust his crotch.

Envy swirls in my belly as I think of him fucking her. I want to be in her place.

He picks up a crop next and starts swatting her ass while she continues to fondle herself with her tongue sticking out.

"Ow!" she cries after the crop lands particularly hard against a buttock.

He strikes her again.

"Ow!"

"I told you to keep that tongue out," he tells her, grabbing a nipple and pulling it hard.

"*Detener!*"

"Wuss," I mutter beneath my breath.

"Lay down," the Dom instructs, setting aside the crop. "Take off the thong and spread your legs so everyone can see your pussy."

I don't want to see her goods, but I don't want to miss a thing he does to her.

He hands her a dildo. "You can fuck yourself but no coming until I say you can."

She works the dildo into herself. He unbinds her breasts and pulls her toward him so that her head hangs off the edge of the bench. He undoes his buckle and unzips his pants.

Yum, I silently purr when he pulls out his stiff cock.

If I had arrived at the club earlier I might have had the chance to pair with him. If only I had known this guy existed...

He places his cock between Carmen's breasts, which he pushes together. While he fucks her tits, she fucks herself with the dildo and rubs her clit.

"I'm going to come, *Maestro,*" she mumbles.

He grabs her hands and has her hold her tits in place. The dildo remains in her pussy while he thrusts faster. He pulls out just before coming and sprays his cum over her orbs. Reaching for the dildo, he works it in and out of her.

"Can I, *Maestro? Por favor?*" she pleads.

"*Puedes.*"

With a grunt, she comes, spasming on the bench, a foot slipping beneath her.

"*Gracias, Maestro,*" she sighs.

"Again," he says.

"What's that?"

He places her hand on the dildo. "Make yourself come again."

I watch as he replaces his cock and pants while Carmen fucks herself some more with the dildo. He pulls her knees further apart to expand the view between her legs. It takes several minutes for her to pant her way to a second orgasm, aided by some heavy clit petting.

"Get up," he says, pulling her up by the hair after she lays still for several beats.

He seems to have just the right amount of roughness to his movements, not too much that it appears uncontrolled but enough that Carmen winces as she gets to her feet.

"Bend down and grab your ankles," he orders.

She does, and I can see her pussy lips beneath her ass. He's not done with her yet?

He rubs her moist folds. "Look at all this slut juice."

She murmurs when he caresses her clit and groans when he sinks his fingers into her twat.

"Oh my god, can I come again?" she asks.

How is she so damn lucky?

"Yes," he answers.

As I watch her twitch coming a third time, I resolve to get a taste of this Dom for myself. I can't remember the last time I've wanted something this badly. At the moment, I want it more than a chance to go down to Mammoth.

And I usually get what I want.

Chapter 5

Casey

NEEDING TO CALM MYSELF, I light a cigarette outside the club. If anyone told me it was illegal to smoke near a public building, I'd claim ignorance and put out my cigarette.

A man I don't recognize walks out. Once I had fixed on the Dom playing with Carmen, I didn't pay attention to anyone else. I watch as the man walks toward a parked car. Soon after, the Dom emerges and seems headed toward another car that had started its engine.

"Hey," I call out to him.

The man pauses but doesn't stop.

"I said 'hey,'" I try again.

Without turning around, he replies, "I don't smoke."

I quickly drop my cigarette and grind it out before catching up to him. "You new to the club?"

He continues across the street. "Not really."

"You play elsewhere?"

"Yes."

"Like where?"

This time he stops, ending up next to a large idling SUV, and faces me. "Why are you asking?"

"Just curious. I saw you with Carmen. You looked really experienced."

"That's because I am."

He opens the backseat door and starts to get in the vehicle.

"Wait!" I exclaim.

He pauses.

"You coming back tomorrow?" I ask. "The club was kind of quiet tonight, but it'll probably pick up tomorrow night. You should check it out then."

His expression is impassive. Is he always this standoffish?

"I'll think about it," is all he says before getting in the car and closing the door.

I watch the car pull away from the curb and drive off. I puff up my cheeks and blow out a sigh. A car starting behind me startles me, so I decide to get off the road and head over to my own car, where Chase is waiting.

I had hoped to get the Dom's name, but he was clearly not interested in me, which is kind of a rare experience. Maybe he likes the more curvy women like Carmen.

But he stared at *me*, not Carmen, when he was sitting at that table. Had he changed his mind after being with Carmen? Was he playing hard to get? Did he have split personalities?

At least he left open the possibility of returning to the club tomorrow night. And if he doesn't show, maybe it's for the best. I noticed his expensive clothes and that he was being chauffeured. Rich people can be obnoxious. I would know because I am one.

I spend the night trying to put him out of my head, but I can't. Simply recalling the way he stared at me makes me shiver. I end up pulling out my vibrator and come multiple times imagining myself in Carmen's place beneath his flogger.

The following day, I can't wait to go back to the club in the evening. Brunch with my mom and dad passes agonizingly slow.

"You'll get fat if you eat too much of that," my mom remarks as the waiter sets down a plate of French toast with mascarpone filling and topped with sliced organic strawberries and powdered sugar.

"It's brunch," I reply as I look skeptically at my mother's salad. Who has salad for brunch?

I cut into the French toast with zest. "Besides, I plan to work it off on the slopes."

Dad looks up from his paper. "What is it you said you were going to do?"

Mom shakes her head. "I don't get why so many Californians like to go skiing. I thought this state was all about the beach scene. And, frankly, I'm disappointed in the beaches here in Northern California."

"Maybe you could go to Hawaii. Invite the Bradys."

"Just us? Can't you come?"

"I'll try to make it, though I have important work that needs to get wrapped up."

Not interested in going to Hawaii with the Bradys, I say, "I have to be back at school in less than two weeks."

"So what if you miss a few days? It's not like you need to get good grades. In fact, you really don't need a college degree once you marry Kenton."

I grind my teeth into a bite of French toast.

"By the way, how did it go last night with Kenton?" my mom asks between sips of her cappuccino. "You didn't come home till late, so I take it that it went pretty well."

"Honestly, I didn't feel any chemistry between us," I answer.

"Give it time."

"It could take forever and still not happen."

My dad interjects, "Chemistry is overrated. It's nothing but overactive hormones, and you don't need it for marriage."

"I already said I don't know that I'll ever want to get married."

"Who wouldn't want to marry Kenton Brady? He's a good-looking young man, he's confident, and he's got a bright future ahead of him."

"There are a lot of good-looking guys with money and bright futures."

"But Kenton is special."

"You mean special to you and your business dealings." I do air quotes around the word business.

Sensing the tension escalating, my mom puts a hand on my dad's before he can respond. She turns to me. "What else are you hoping for in Kenton?"

I swirl a bite of French toast in the syrup on my plate. "More personality, maybe. A backbone."

"Backbone?" my dad exclaims in surprise. "You won't find anyone more confident than him."

I meet his gaze. "He's arrogant, sure, but that doesn't make him brave."

"You don't know what you're talking about."

"I saw it with my own eyes. We were in the same restaurant in South Bend. His buddies started picking on these two Muslim girls. He didn't do anything to try and stop them."

"It's not his job to police his friends. Besides, you get hardened in our line of business."

"More reason not to marry Kenton, then."

"You're not even giving him a chance," my father growls. "This is the best match for you."

"I get that it's the best match for you, but it isn't for me."

He pounds the table. "Stop being so entitled!"

I can't believe my ears. "I'm being entitled because I want to decide for myself who I want to marry, if I want to marry?"

"It's not as if I'm asking you to marry some poor slob off the streets."

"You can't make me marry Kenton!"

My mom tries to calm the air. "I think we should finish our brunch and talk about this later."

Ignoring her, my father continues to address me. "I've given you everything you've ever wanted. I'm paying for your tuition to Notre Dame, your ski trips, the clothes you're wearing. What have you done for this family?"

I throw down my fork and stand up. "Then don't pay for everything! I'll find a way to support myself!"

"Casey!" my mom pleads. "You know that's not what your father meant."

"All he cares about is me marrying Kenton. Maybe he thinks living a life of luxury while my husband fucks women half his age behind my back is good enough for me. Well, it's not!"

With that, I whirl around and storm out. I go in search of Chase, who has my car keys.

"I'm going for a drive," I tell him.

Wordlessly, he hands over the keys and follows me to the garage. He gets into his car. I hate that he has to go wherever I go.

I don't know where I'm headed. I only know that I want to get away from my parents, from my stupid, suffocating life.

A call comes in from Hannah. "Hey, girl, you want to go shopping?"

"We went shopping two days ago," I reply.

"So? What does that have to do with shopping *to-day*?"

"I don't feel like shopping."

"Then how about we make it a spa day?"

"We did that the other day too."

I don't want to go shopping or have a spa day. I want to vent my frustrations on the slopes, something impactful, to get the blood pumping. All my friends ever want to do is go shopping, get a facial, lounge by the pool, or if it's later in the evening, go out for drinks or clubbing. I need more excitement in my life than that.

What I need is the right Dom.

I can't wait for Club de Sade to open.

Chapter 6

Casey

I CAN BARELY CONTAIN my excitement when I see *him* here at the club, but I have to play it cool. I'm not convinced the guy is interested in me, so I don't want to come across too eager. But he's going to be mine tonight. Nothing is going to stand in the way of that.

Except maybe Carmen.

The olive-skinned beauty has large breasts—probably enlarged—and her red bustier makes her look like Jessica Rabbit. She has on bright red come-get-me platform heels and a flirty school girl skirt that barely covers her voluptuous backside. With dismay, I watch Carmen make her way toward the guy.

"Shit," I curse and hurry in the same direction.

"So you've come back for more, big boy?" Carmen drawls as she puts a foot up on the chair next to where the man had seated himself.

"Hey!" I greet, sitting on the edge of the table before him. "Glad you decided to come back."

In surprise, Carmen glances between us, trying to make out the connection. "You two know each other?"

"Yeah," I reply while he answers, "No."

"We talked," I clarify.

"We did. I told you I don't smoke," the man says.

Ignoring Carmen's smirk, I say, "I don't smoke all the time. Rarely, in fact. Yesterday just happened to be stressful."

"Stressful?" Carmen echoes. "Wasn't it your birthday yesterday?"

"Yeah, well, birthdays can be stressful."

"So you're, like, legal now?"

I frown. Carmen knows that no one under eighteen is allowed in the club. But maybe the Dom likes age play?

"I turned twenty-one," I say.

Carmen raises a brow as if she isn't sure she believes me. "I like your corset thing. It makes your breasts look...cute."

Suppressing a scowl, I smile and reply, "Thanks. And those heels are really killing it for you. No one would know you're barely five feet tall."

I don't want to get into a catfight in front of the Dom, who watches our exchange with a tinge of amusement, but it's too hard to resist.

Deciding not to continue with Carmen, however, I turn to the Dom. "You playing tonight?"

Warmth churns inside my belly when he looks at me.

"Possibly."

"Why come if you're not going to play?" Carmen asks. She leans in toward him, giving him a closer view of her cleavage. "I'd make it worth your while."

The man looks from Carmen back to me. I stare into his eyes, telling him with my gaze that he's better off choosing me. He seems intrigued by what I have to 'say.'

"I'll give the birthday girl a gift and play," he says.

Yes! I want to do a fist pump.

Carmen's face darkens as she says to me, "Looks like you'll get your wish of having had every cock that walks through the door."

Though I want to bitch-slap Carmen, I bite back a retort. Instead, I'm going to be gracious in my victory.

Ignoring Carmen, I ask the Dom, "Which stall do you like?"

He looks over the options before replying, "The one with the wooden bench."

Reluctantly, Carmen gets off the table, but she bends over to whisper into his ear before leaving. "When you're done with jailbait and want a real woman, I'm always game for you, big boy."

Carmen doesn't lower her voice much, so I hear every word. Channeling Aleisha, I tell myself to let it go, imagining Aleisha telling me, *Carmen's just jealous.*

And who wouldn't be? I think to myself with a smile. I just scored one of the most delicious Doms to walk into the club.

A server wearing a bunny outfit comes by and sets down a mug before him.

I address the server. "Can I get a coffee too?"

"This is tea," the Dom says.

"I didn't know they served tea here," I say, surprised.

I look at him curiously. "I don't think I've ever met a man who drinks tea. Most guys go for the harder stuff. They'd think tea was a wussy drink."

"Maybe the guys you know feel they have something to prove with what they drink. I don't."

I like his response. I remember hearing my brother say, when asked if he wanted a cocktail, that real men drank beer. Guys like Jake or Kenton would balk at drinking tea. Alcohol would be best, but coffee would at least be "manlier" than tea. So, in a way, it takes serious *cojones* for a guy to be seen drinking tea in public.

Realizing I don't even know the name of the guy I'm about to play with, I say, "My name's Casey. What's yours?"

"You know how to address me," he replies after sipping his tea.

"I do?"

He gives me a look suggesting I should know better.

"Sir?" I guess.

He nods. "What's your preferred safe word?"

"Do I need one?" I return flirtatiously.

He raises a brow. "You always this reckless?"

"It's kind of exciting without one."

"What's your middle name?"

I wrinkle my nose. "I don't like my middle name."

"What is it? And don't make me ask a third time. I don't have the patience for disobedient subs."

With a pout, I relent. "Maeve."

"That's your safe word. What are your hard limits?"

"I don't do scat play, but that's about it."

With a tinge of skepticism, he asks, "Everything else is fair game?"

I shrug. "Why not?"

"Have you tried everything else?"

"No, but there has to be a first time so I can decide whether or not I like it."

He leans back in his chair and studies me. "You're very trusting."

My voice comes out husky without trying. "You seem like a guy who knows what he's doing."

"You can't know for sure based on what little you saw yesterday."

"I've got a good intuition about you."

"What else does your intuition tell you about me?"

"That you could be the Dom I've been looking for."

"What if your intuition's wrong?"

"It's not."

He gives an almost a smirk, as if he's disputing my claim. Why would he do that?

"How long have you been in the scene?" he asks.

"Almost two years."

"You're a little young for me."

"That doesn't mean I can't be a good sub for you."

He seems to accept my response. He sets down his tea. "Let's find out."

Chapter 7

Kai

S HE'S TRYING TO HIDE her giddiness, but I can sense it. I felt the intensity of her gaze—*I want you*, it said—before I chose to play with her. I saw how she had perked up after my decision. She hops off the table with eagerness.

"I'll go slip into something more interesting," Casey says.

"That won't be necessary," I tell her.

"It won't take long. It's just a bottom that matches—"

My stare cuts off the rest of her sentence. Realizing she isn't being a good sub, she lowers her gaze.

"Sorry, Sir," she murmurs.

I grasp her jaw, firmly enough to make her gasp. "You said you could be a good sub for me."

"I am," she replies with all the confidence of her youth.

She doesn't know what she doesn't know.

Releasing her, I nod toward our stall.

She steps in that direction, then checks to make sure that it's okay with me before continuing. I could make her crawl on all fours behind me, but I don't want to jump into humiliation play right away.

Once in the stall, I instruct her to straddle the bench and sit down. I look over the offerings on the wall and shelves. Picking up a collar with the word SLUT on it, I show it to her.

"That you, princess?" I ask.

"If you want it to be, Sir," she replies.

"Is what Carmen said true about you having every cock that walks through the door?"

She rolls her eyes. "Half the men who come here don't even play with women."

"But you've had a lot of cock."

"I've tried different partners, but that's only because I haven't found a good Dom yet. Maybe tonight's my lucky night."

She gives me a smoldering gaze. Poor thing has no idea what she's inviting.

"Oh, you're lucky all right, princess," I say and have her take the collar. "Put it on."

She buckles the collar around her neck. "I hope that's not just talk."

I reach for a cord of rope. "You always challenge your Doms like that?"

"No, Sir. It's just that I've met so many guys who talk a big game, and that's all it is: talk. But you strike me as the strong, silent type, so I'm hoping you can deliver."

"What if you get more than you bargained for?"

"Better than being disappointed."

I bend her arms behind her back and, straddling the bench behind her, start tying her forearms together. The perfume she wears isn't bad, though I prefer a more natural fragrance. "What kind of play do you like the most?"

"I don't have a favorite. I like all kinds."

"What have you done?"

"Impact play, age play, wax play, breath play," she lists.

"Have you done watersports?"

"I'd like to, one day, with the right Dom."

"Electroplay?"

"Haven't tried that yet, but I'm open to it."

"Multiple partners?" I inquire.

"I've been in threesomes. An MMF and FMF."

"No lesbian play?"

"It's not really my thing. I prefer cock—real cocks."

Done with binding her forearms, I grip her by the chin and make her look toward a stall along a wall adjacent to ours. A man and woman there are having sex doggy-style.

"You had that cock before?" I ask.

"I can't tell who it is."

I slap her, hard enough to get her full attention and a little extra to show her I'm not to be messed with. From our viewpoint, we can see three quarters of the man's face. "Don't lie to me, princess."

"Yes," she says clearly.

"What did you think of his cock?"

"The cock was all right."

"Just all right? It looks nice and long from here."

"He's a one-note Dom, so it doesn't matter how many inches he has."

I fist my hand into her hair and yank her head back so that I can look into her eyes. "How many cocks have you had?"

"Why do you want to know?"

Forcing my hand down into her top, I pinch and pull her nipple.

"Ow, ow, ow," she cries, squirming.

"Good subs don't make me repeat my questions."

"I haven't kept count, Sir."

I twist her nipple.

"At least twenty!"

"Or thirty?"

She squeals. "Maybe!"

I release her nipple. "So you've been a busy little slut. Your daddy know you're this naughty?"

After catching her breath, she rolls her eyes back to look at me. "He does now."

Damn, I think before answering, "Cute. Does princess have daddy issues?"

She falters for a moment, the look on her face telling me the answer.

"I'm looking for a daddy who'll spoil his little girl," she says coyly.

"I bet your real dad already does that for you. I'm not the spoiling kind. I'm the punishing kind, especially with spoiled brats."

To my surprise, she licks her lips at that. Needing space to keep my cool, I stand up and take a flogger off the wall. She watches me with an excited gleam in her eyes.

I turn her head back toward the couple in the other stall where the man is pistoning his hips hard and fast. "Did you fuck that rough when you were with him?"

"Yes," Casey acknowledges.

"You liked it?"

"Yes."

"Is daddy's little princess a pain slut?"

She turns her bright green eyes on me again. "You should find out for yourself."

"I will," I say, half to myself.

Holding the flogger in front of her, I let the tails caress their way from her breast to her bare shoulder before I pull back and slap the flogger against her thigh.

"Thank you, Sir."

I hadn't specified that she had to thank me. Maybe she can be a good sub after all.

Which doesn't matter, I remind myself. Good or not, she's going be the leverage I need to get my asset back.

"You wet yet?" I ask after warming her body with the flogger some more.

"A little," she says.

"Spread your legs wider."

When she does, I strike her crotch with the flogger. With her jeans protecting the area, she barely yelps. I land the flogger between her legs several times.

"Mmmmm," she murmurs.

I spank her pussy a few more times before, standing behind her, I place her in a chokehold using the handle of the flogger.

"I assume you know that you have to ask permission to come," I state.

"Yes, Sir."

I pull the flogger tighter against her till she starts to squirm, pushing off on her heels in a bid to keep the handle from crushing her neck. I let her go. She coughs and gasps in air.

Wordlessly, I wait for her response. When she's caught her breath, she looks at me with a little bit of bewilderment but also some excitement.

"Are you wetter now?" I ask.

"Yes."

"I want to be able to see it through your jeans."

"I can get real wet for you, Sir. It just takes a little while for the juices to get flowing. That's where you come in."

"You don't need me. You've got this." I tap her temple. At her frown, I say, "Don't tell me princess is a dumb blonde."

"I like action."

"Did you know some women can make themselves orgasm with thought alone?"

"Lucky them. If I could do that, I probably wouldn't need to be here."

I acknowledge that ever since discovering BDSM for myself, it's easier to get aroused. Just the sight of her with her arms pinioned behind her is enough to stir warmth in my groin. I don't need full frontal shots of naked women with oversized tits. A fully clothed woman in expert shibari is far more evocative.

"Give it a try," I tell Casey.

"Give what a try?"

"Make yourself wet with thought."

She pouts as if I've just told her to practice her math sets. "Don't you want to flog my pussy some more?"

"Don't you want to do as you're told?" I scold.

At that, she purses her lips in resignation and closes her eyes. I watch her, amused that something as simple as using her imagination could bother her. If I were training her, I'd have her do a lot more mental exercises. It might be more painful for her than bastinado.

After a minute or so, she peeks at me, probably hoping for a sign that she can come.

Prying her knees further apart, I look at her crotch. "I don't see anything."

"It's not working for me."

"Try harder."

With a sigh, she closes her eyes again.

"What are you thinking about?" I ask.

"I'm thinking how in a minute you'll show me you're a man of action, not just talk—or thought."

I slap her sharply across the cheek. She stares at me wide-eyed with a flash of how-dare-you indignation. She really is a princess.

Grabbing her hair, I yank her head back and look down at her. "Maybe your issue isn't that you haven't found a good Dom. It's that you're a piss-poor sub."

"I'm sorry, Sir," she apologizes.

She looks and sounds sincere. I twist my hand into her hair, pulling on her scalp till her brow furrows and lips remain parted.

"I like action," she reiterates.

"All right. Since it was your birthday yesterday, I'll give you action. No guarantees that you'll like it, though."

Chapter 8

Casey

ANTICIPATION SURGES THROUGH ME. I haven't been this excited since my early days in BDSM. The slaps to the face sting, but I like them. I know I'm being a bit of a brat, but I want to make sure he doesn't go too easy on me. Based on the tone of his voice, I don't think I have to worry about that. And I'm glad I successfully goaded him into action. I don't have the patience to think my way to an orgasm.

He pushes my face down into the bench, then lets go of my hair to unzip my top. Grabbing my hair again, he pulls me back into a sitting position. I relish the pull on my scalp. With my merry widow off, he has access to my breasts, which he flogs until my skin tingles all over. This is more like it.

He alternates between flogging and slapping my breasts for several minutes before setting down the flogger. Straddling the bench behind me, he reaches for both breasts. He toys with my nipples, gently tugging and rolling each between his thumb and forefinger.

"I've creamed my panties for you, Sir," I tell him.

"You think that's enough to please me?" he returns.

Using my nipples, he pulls my breasts in all different directions before mauling and slapping them. I yelp when one of the smacks glances off my nipple. He grabs the hardened nub and adds to the pain by twisting and pulling. I fall back against him with a cry. Sitting down, he holds me in place with his other arm while I squirm, but there's no place for me to go. The more I try to get away from his grip on my nipple, the more I aid his efforts.

"Shit!" I squeal. Is he trying to pull my nipple off?

Just when I think I might need my safe word with this guy after all, he releases my nipple and finishes with a sharp smack to the side of my breast.

In a husky voice, he says, "What do you say?"

"Thank you, Sir," I whimper.

"Now for the other nipple."

Shit. I brace myself. But he doesn't go for the nipple right away. Instead, he massages my breast, his deft fingers kneading the pliant flesh.

"Natural. I like that," he says.

At one point in my life I had considered breast augmentation, but I'm glad I never went through with it.

After he has me relaxed a bit, he starts on the nipple torture. I try to grit my teeth, but the fucker is hard on my poor nub. My screams draw the attention of everyone in the club. But I can't give in and use my safe word. Not this early. Not after I boasted that I might not need one.

"You can fuck me now, Sir," I say during a reprieve.

"You haven't earned cock yet," he says. "And don't try to top from the bottom."

He resumes pinching, pulling, and twisting my nipple until I wish I had never been born with nipples.

"Let's see how wet you are now," he says before cupping a hand to my crotch. "You've soaked through your jeans. Good."

Even though I'm not looking forward to wearing soggy jeans back home, I'm glad that he's pleased. He rubs me between the legs, and I'd give just about anything to have the barrier of my jeans removed. I press myself against his hand, trying to feel more of him through the fabric.

When it seems like he might just tease me like this forever, I plead, "Please put your hand down my pants."

"What are you offering in exchange?"

In exchange? There're dozens of guys who would happily shove their hand down my pants in exchange for nothing.

"I could suck you off real good, Sir."

"Already plan on having you do that."

"I'd let you into my ass."

"Better. Would you suck off five cocks for me?"

My pussy throbs. "Yes."

"Would you go down on Carmen?"

I bristle. I don't want that at all, but I want to please my Dom. I want his hand on my pussy, flesh to flesh.

"I'd do it for you, Sir," I answer, hoping he won't actually make me do it.

He undoes the button of my jeans and slowly pulls the zipper down. I practically pant from excitement as I watch his fingers disappear into my jeans and wish I had worn a looser pair, but I sigh with contentment when he nestles his fingers between my jeans and my lace underwear. Lightly, he strokes my clit through the lace. I moan softly, remaining as still as possible, fearing that any movement might make him stop. Wetness gushes into my panties. He hasn't even done that much to me yet, but it's the prospect of what he can do, all that potential present in his tone, his controlled touch, his calm confidence that's driving me crazy.

When he pulls his hand from my pants, I whimper, wishing he would continue caressing me but excited to see what he will do next. He pushes my face down into the bench again before getting up, then pulls me to the end of the bench till my ass rounds the edge. Grabbing another cord of rope, he binds my neck to the bench. With my face turned toward the club, I can see that most of the viewers are watching me. He pulls my jeans down to my thighs, revealing my underwear and a small tattoo in the shape of handcuffs at the top of my right ass cheek.

"Fancy panties for a fancy princess," he comments before baring my rump. He runs his thumb over my tattoo. "How long have you had this?"

"Got it on my birthday last year."

Dropping his hand, he gives one cheek a swat, then spanks the other several times. I purr with satisfaction. Picking up the flogger, he warms up my backside.

"Your ass gets red fast," he notes.

I wiggle it for him.

He smirks before landing the tails sharply against a buttock. This time it has more sting. After a few more wallops, he switches to a crop.

"Which impact toy do you like the most?" he asks.

"I'm not sure," I answer truthfully.

"Let's find your favorite tonight. Since you turned twenty-one, we'll do twenty-one strikes per instrument. You'll do the counting."

"Yes, Sir."

He whips the crop across an ass cheek, the strike sharper than the flogger.

"One," I count.

The second slap is even sharper, causing me to jump, except that I am bound to the bench. My arms, still tied behind my back, are getting a little sore.

"Two."

He takes his time, striking only when the sting from the previous blow has begun to fade. As a result, my ass has no relief from the burn, but I take it in stride, the nectar of my desire continuing to flow. I savor each and every time the crop connects with my ass. It hurts, but I pride myself on having a high pain threshold. After he's delivered twenty-one with the crop, he reaches between my legs, lightly grazing my moist folds. I wait for him to touch me more significantly, like rub my clit or sink his fingers into my pussy, but he only tugs on my labia. I feel only the slightest sensation against my clit.

"You like the crop?" he asks as he continues to feel me up without touching my clit.

"Yes, Sir."

"Ready to try something else?"

"Yes, Sir."

To my dismay, he stands up. That's all the foreplay I'm going to get before the next round of pain?

"I like it when you touch my clit, Sir," I tell him.

"I know you do," he replies as he looks at two different paddles hanging on the wall, a plain wooden one and a leather one with a heart imprint.

A little impatient, I inquire, "Are you the type of Dom who skimps on foreplay?"

"For that, I'm going to go with the heavier paddle."

Shit. There's no manipulating or getting one over on this guy.

After removing the paddle from the wall, he holds it in front of me. It looks to be about quarter of an inch thick. I have never been spanked with anything that thick before.

"Give it a kiss to show your appreciation," he instructs.

Doing as told, I kiss the harbinger of pain. He goes to stand behind me and caresses the curve of my ass. I brace myself and wait. And wait.

"Sir?"

"Beg me to spank you."

"Please spank me, Sir."

"Why?"

"Because I've been a bad girl."

"Is that because you're a spoiled princess?"

"Yes."

"Beg some more."

"I need to be spanked. I deserve to be spanked—"

The paddle strikes me hard. And because I'm busy talking, I don't brace myself. The blow would've sent me over the bench if I wasn't tied down to it.

"Holy shit!" I exclaim.

"My subs don't get to swear," he says. "Curse again and I'll double your count."

"Yes, Sir. One, Sir."

"Keep begging for the paddle."

"I need you to spank me badly, Sir. I've been so naughty, so spoiled."

"Your daddy spoil you?"

I see Carmen in the audience smirking.

"Yes, Sir."

"How?"

"He gives me everything: clothes, vacations, cars."

"Cars? You have more than one car?"

"I got my first one when I was sixteen but it got totaled."

"How did that happen?"

"I was texting and didn't notice how close I was to the car in front of me. When I slammed on the brakes, the car behind me knocked me into the car in front. Instead of getting the car fixed, I asked my dad if I could have a new one."

"And daddy came through for you."

"Yes, Sir."

The next blow slams my hip bones into the bench.

"Two," I mumble.

At least the paddle delivers a thudding pain, which I prefer over stinging pain.

"We're still at one," he says. "That was a bonus spank for driving distracted. This one is number two."

The next one is bruising.

"Shit!"

The word falls from my mouth before I can even think. I pray he hasn't heard me, but of course he has.

Chapter 9

Kai

"WHAT DID I SAY about swearing?" I ask.

"Not to. I'm sorry, Sir. I'll do better," she says in earnest.

"For your sake, I hope so."

I tap the paddle against her ass before pulling it back and smacking her several times in succession till she chokes on her own gasps.

"How many are we at?" I ask.

"Eight, Sir."

I take my time with the next few spanks, relishing the quiver of her buttocks after each impact.

"Your ass is going to be sore for a while after we're done," I remark, noting that her whole ass glows crimson.

"I'd like that, Sir," she murmurs.

When I get to twenty, I give her a reprieve. Dropping to a knee, I reach between her thighs and fondle her. I make sure to tease her clit nice and good this time. She moans and grows wetter.

"Fu—yesss," she groans when I sink two of my fingers into her hot, wet snatch.

The slurping, slapping sounds of my motions mix with her grunts and gasps of pleasure. Her pussy grasps at my fingers. She is definitely fuckable material, but we aren't there yet.

Withdrawing my hand, I press my fingers to her lips. Without hesitating, she takes in my digits and sucks. I feel a corresponding tug at my groin.

"You taste good?" I ask her.

"Yes, Sir. You should try some."

I grin at her impish response before pulling out my fingers and wiping the saliva on her cheek.

"Let's finish the other half," I say.

Her shoulders sag, but she doesn't protest.

"Twenty-one!" she counts diligently after the paddle smacks her on both ass cheeks.

"Was anyone hurt in your car accident?" I ask before paddling her again.

"The woman I hit had whiplash. Unh! Twenty-two."

I strike her rump. "And you?"

"Twenty-three! I was okay."

"You plan on texting while driving again?"

I whack her again.

"Twenty-four! No, Sir!"

"Your daddy ever punish you?"

She fists her hands after the next spank. "Twenty-five. Not really."

"Then we have a lot of ground to make up."

With the next blow, she has to catch her breath. "T-Twenty-six."

"You're doing good, princess," I compliment. I like that she hasn't complained so far and give her a few lighter smacks.

"You remember your safe word?" I ask when we reach thirty.

"Yes, Sir. Thirty-one!"

"What is it?"

She doesn't respond till I bring the paddle down on her. "Thirty-two! It's Maeve."

"Couldn't hear you," I lie.

"Thirty-three! My safe word is Maeve!"

"I push my subs to their limits, so it's important to remember your safe word. Got that?"

"Yes, Sir. Thirty-four! Have all your subs needed their safe words? Thirty-five!"

"Yes."

"Thirty-six!"

She's been wiggling around on the bench as if trying to shake off the burn in her ass, but I've been keeping an eye on her expressions. She isn't close to her limit, and we are almost done with the paddling. The cane might prove to be a different story.

"Thirty-seven...thirty-eight...thirty-nine..."

"Louder," I command.

"Forty!"

The next one makes her swear, and the last one knocks the breath from her.

"Forty-two," she finishes, her voice weaker.

It doesn't seem like she bruises easily, though parts of her ass have a purplish hue. I set aside the paddle.

"You took your punishment well," I tell her.

"Thank you, Sir."

"It's deserving of some reward."

From the shelf, I select a remote-controlled vibrating egg, new and still in its packaging. I take it out and test it to see that it works. It does. I look to Casey and see that her eyes shimmer with anticipation. She has pretty eyes. Her mother's eyes. Liam is a good-looking man, but Casey resembles her mother more.

Crouching down, I slide the egg into Casey and turn it on to its lowest setting.

"Mmm," she purrs.

"No coming without permission," I tell her.

"Yes, Sir."

I go for the cane next and see her frown. "What's the matter? Not a fan?"

"It's not my favorite."

I smack the cane into my palm. "It is for me."

Lightly, I tap the cane against her ass. "I like the variety of sensations it offers. It can sting like this."

I whip it quickly against her, making her gasp.

"One!"

"Or it can deliver a heavy thud."

She grunts with the next blow. "Two!"

"Then there's the marks a cane leaves."

"Three!"

She clenches and unclenches her hands.

"We could leave some nice train tracks here."

I swat her left buttock twice.

"Four! Five!"

I crank the vibrator up two notches.

"And a set here," I say, swatting her right buttock twice.

When she doesn't respond, I ask, "Where's my count?"

"Seven?"

"Since you're not sure, let's start over."

She groans. I strike her three times in succession.

She writhes on the bench before saying, "One, two and three."

"Or we could go for crisscrossing marks," I muse aloud of the potentially more damaging strokes. "I could carve your ass up good with an angry, messy caning."

"Yes, Sir."

Not wanting to go too extreme on our first play together, I avoid crossing my strikes. After several more applications of the cane, she has tears in her eyes. On the ninth strike, I expect her to use her safe word, but she's stronger than she looks. I reward her by increasing the vibrations of the egg and allow her to enjoy it for a few minutes without inflicting the cane on her.

"Can I come, Sir?" she asks.

"Not till we're done."

I whip her ass.

"Ten!" she whimpers.

The next one makes her scream loud enough for others in the middle of their own scene to stop and look our way. After the twelfth smack, I wonder if I will have to tie her up more to keep her in place. She pummels the ground with her feet on the thirteenth blow.

"Sh—!" she almost swears at one point.

Her derrierre, crimson from the paddling, now bears streaks of deeper red from the caning.

"You should see how incredible your ass looks," I say when we are nearly done.

She cries out each time as she counted eighteen, nineteen, then twenty.

"Can I come now?" she says, her voice trembling.

In response, I crank the vibrations to its highest setting. "Yes."

With a silent cry, she comes undone, bucking and flailing against the bench. I ease the vibrations down to a simmer.

"Want to come again?" I ask.

"Yes, sir," she answers after a shaky breath.

Still holding the remote in one hand, I grab the flogger with the other and place the handle between her thighs. "Make yourself come."

She grinds herself against the handle, rubbing her clit over the flared bottom. I increase the vibrations.

She gives a rapturous groan and bears down harder on the flogger, grunting and grinding her way to her climax. I send her over the top by turning the vibrations to its highest setting. Her body strains, then shakes.

"Oh, *god...*" she squeals, her buttocks lifted as if trying to escape me, though it was the egg inside her that's causing the overwhelm of sensations, and she can't escape that.

I keep her in that elevated state of orgasm for several beats, with her eyes clenched shut, her body taut, before releasing her by turning down the vibrations and eventually off.

A final shiver goes through as I extract the egg. I gaz at her ass, admiring my artwork. I hadn't expected to go as hard as I did with a partner I've never played with before, but she didn't use her safe word. I can't help but feel a little impressed.

Seeing a tendril of hair has fallen between her lips, I lift it out of her mouth. "Not bad for a princess."

Casey lays still on the bench, her eyes still closed. "Thank you, sir."

"They have any aftercare products here?"

"Aloe vera but it sometimes stings," she murmurs as I undo the rope around her neck. "I have my own stuff anyway."

"Happy birthday, princess," I say after untying her arms.

She straightens but doesn't pull up her panties and jeans, still bunched above her knees. "We're done?"

I pick up her corset and hand it to her. "Yes."

She wraps it around herself and zips it up. "I thought you were going to make me suck you off?"

I eye her lips. My cock would look nice between them, but I don't want to give away too much our first time together. "Maybe another time."

She perks up. "So we get to do this again?"

I set the implements I used into a basket marked for cleaning before heading out. "No promises."

At that, she frowns. Quickly, she pulls up her clothes, wincing when the fabric passes her ass, and follows me.

"Why not?" she demands. "Wasn't I a good sub?"

"You were decent," I acknowledge.

"I was better than decent."

I don't respond and continue walking.

"Hey!" she calls.

Whipping around, I grab her by the throat. "I don't respond to 'hey.'"

"You just did."

I squeeze tighter.

Her eyes widen. "Sir! I meant sir."

I release her and turn back around.

"I can do better," she assures me. "I'm just a little out of practice. I've been at school for the last few months. I just need to get back in the groove."

I collect my jacket from where I had left it on the back of my chair, prepared to call it a night. Or maybe I'll stop by The Lotus where I can take care of my wood.

Casey steps in front of me. "Can I buy you a drink?"

Looking into her bright and eager eyes, I have to smile to myself. I have her right where I want.

Chapter 10

Casey

I 'VE NEVER HAD TO buy a guy a drink before. Men offer to buy *me* drinks. But I can't let this guy get away without knowing when I'd see him again. My ass burns like never before, and I love it. The orgasms have been among the best I have ever had, even though I've used that exact same type of egg myself.

As he contemplates my question, I start to formulate what I can say to convince him. I don't want to come off desperate, but I have never wanted to be with a guy this much before.

"You scared?" I prompt.

"Of a drink?" he returns, sounding incredulous.

"Yeah."

He stares deep into my eyes. "You want me bad, don't you?"

I balk at his arrogance, even though it is true. Lifting my chin, I reply, "So what if I do? That scare you?"

"Why would that scare me?"

"I don't know. Maybe you're scared that I'm a better sub than you think, that I'll ruin all other subs for you."

"You have no idea what you'd be getting yourself into with me, princess."

"And I could be the one to fulfill all your fantasies."

"You don't even know what they are."

"Only one way to find out. So we doing this drink or not?"

He thinks for a beat, and I suspect he is going to decline, but then he sets his jacket back down.

"Not here," I say, noticing Carmen.

"Where?"

"Want to get something to eat? I'm starving."

He looks at his watch, a sleek black timepiece with a silver or platinum frame. It looks expensive without being ostentatious.

"You have a place in mind? It's past one o'clock."

There aren't any nice restaurants still seating at this hour, though he looks like he has been to his share of fancy restaurants. I furrow my brow in thought. Maybe there is a nice bar still open? But maybe not on a Sunday.

"You like Chinese food?" he asks when I don't come up with anything.

"Yeah," I reply. "Is that what you feel like having?"

"You're the one who's hungry. There's always late-night stuff around Chinatown."

"Great! You want to drive?"

I do *not* want to have to cart around Chase with what might be my only chance to have the guy all to myself.

"Sure."

"Just give me a few minutes."

"I'll be outside."

With almost giddy steps, I head over to Chase. "I'm going to grab something to eat in Chinatown. He's driving. You can follow us, but I do *not* want to have to explain you."

Chase nods as he suppresses a yawn.

I hurry to the changing room, where I pull down my panties and jeans to apply a cooling ointment.

"Damn, girl, that's some serious spanking you got," says Aleisha.

I inspect my backside in the mirror. My ass has never been this red before, and it's clear where the cane landed.

"It'll be days before that goes away," she adds.

"Yeah," I agree.

"You sound like you're happy about that."

"I am. Kind of. There's something about the guy that's so...masterful." I pull my panties and jeans back up and wince. "I mean, he seemed so deliberate in what he was doing. He wasn't inflicting pain just because he could."

Aleisha looks skeptical.

"I don't know quite how to describe it. I mean, yeah, I get off on pain—"

"A little too much maybe?"

"—but I've never felt so turned on before. I guess you had to be there."

"Oh, I was. It is hard to ignore your screams. I saw a good amount of your scene, and I get what you're saying about the guy. You should have seen the way he looked at you. *That* is hot."

"Yeah?"

I bite my bottom lip. This is the Dom I've been looking for.

Aleisha lowers her voice. "Carmen is so jealous. She was seething."

I can't help but smile. "He and I are going to grab something to eat now."

"Damn, you're scoring tonight."

"I know, right? I just wish I had the chance to fully change into my outfit before playing tonight. Now I'm stuck with these jeans."

Aleisha laughs.

After changing my top, I put the merry widow into a locker, slip on my coat, and go to meet the guy outside. I still don't know his name, but I'll get it soon enough.

He is parked in a sleek silver Ferrari, the engine idling as he waits for me. If Carmen saw this, she'd hate on me even more.

"This your usual ride?" I ask after settling into the burgundy-colored leather seat, remembering he didn't have this car the first time we met.

"I don't have a usual ride," he replies as he pulls the car from the curb.

From the corners of my eyes, I see Chase in my car turn on the headlights. 'Sir' seems to notice too.

"So do I get a name now?" I ask.

"Besides 'princess'?"

Is he teasing me or being serious? I can't tell by the tone of his voice.

"I meant *yours.*"

"Jack."

I eye him more closely. For some reason, he doesn't look like a Jack.

"Mine's Casey."

"I know. You told me."

Several beats of silence pass before I ask, "So where're we headed?"

"A noodle place."

"Cool. I bet the Chinese food is really good here in San Francisco."

He glances over at me. "You haven't lived here long?"

"A year, but I'm mostly at school."

"Where's that?"

"Notre Dame."

"Home of 'The Fighting Irish.'"

"Yeah, guess it's kind of cliche that I go there, though the university was founded by a French priest."

"You're Irish?"

"Yeah. You can probably tell by my name: Casey Maeve Callaghan."

"Where did you live before?"

"Boston."

"Why did your family move?"

I'm encouraged that he wants to know more about me. At the beginning, it didn't seem like he was that interested in going anywhere with me.

"My dad wasn't satisfied with the, um, business opportunities there. Too many competitors."

"What does he do?"

"He's in business."

"What kind of business?"

I shift in my seat and look out the window on my side. "Variety of stuff."

"Like what?"

"I don't know exactly. He doesn't talk about it very much to me, probably because he knows I'm not interested."

"Why aren't you interested?"

I shrug. "It sounds boring."

"What about it is boring?"

I turn to look at him. It almost feels like he's grilling me.

"Everything," I reply.

"Give me an example."

I struggle to find an answer. It's true that my dad doesn't talk specifics with me, but I've heard things in passing.

"Like investments or stocks, maybe," I lie. "To me, it's all nerdy, boring stuff."

The words fall from my mouth before I realize maybe that's exactly what Jack does for a living. But he doesn't look affronted. Instead, he stares at me, almost as if he knows I'm lying.

I'm glad when the traffic light turns red and he has to focus his gaze on the road.

"I mean, it's probably because I wasn't ever good at math, and that's why it doesn't interest me," I try to cover myself.

Shit. I sound like a dumbass.

"Are you a stockbroker?" I venture.

"My business is sales and procurement."

"What kind of sales and procurement?"

"Technology and hardware."

We return to sitting in silence. This guy is impossible to flirt with, so I resort to the perfunctory first date questions.

"Were you born here in San Francisco?" I ask while we drive through Chinatown.

"No."

I wait for him to elaborate. When he doesn't, I prompt him. "Somewhere else in California then?"

"I wasn't born in the US."

"Then where?"

Jesus, why is it so hard getting answers out of this guy? I don't get him at all. He agreed to spend more time with me—on what most people would consider a date—but he doesn't seem particularly happy about it.

"I was born in a hospital in Russia," he reveals.

"Really? Did you grow up there?"

"I grew up near Russia, in China."

He pulls up in front of a small mixed-use building in an area situated on the edge of Chinatown and the Italian district of North Beach. We're a stone's throw away from where the strip bars and adult stores are, and I don't see any valet options here. But we manage to find a parking spot—probably because of the later hour—which feels like winning the lottery in this city.

"When did you move to the US?" I ask.

He turns to me after putting the car in park. "Look, princess, this isn't a date. I'm not looking for a relationship or a long-term partner. You said you could fulfill all my fantasies. I want to know how."

Chapter 11

Kai

S HE BALKS AT MY frankness, then seems slightly disappointed. Casey Callaghan is probably used to men fawning over her and eating out of her hand. But even though she's pretty in the classic American sense, she's not my type for a variety of reasons, not the least of which is the fact that she's the daughter of my enemy.

Carmen is more my type physically. I like brunettes and women with more backside. And I like them less naive and spoiled. But for now, Casey is my goal.

I get out of the car and see that her bodyguard has parked her car not too far from us. My men, Xiao and Ray, have pulled up across the street.

Normally I'd open the passenger door for a woman, but that's what Casey's used to. Still in the car, she doesn't budge. I cross my arms. Probably realizing

I'm not opening the door for her, she gets out on her own. I nod toward the restaurant. She opens the door and walks in.

The establishment looks like it opened in the 70s and hasn't changed since. Tables with Formica tops and plastic chairs fill the space to the brim. A half dozen college students have pushed their tables together on one side of the restaurant. A pair of cops sit on the other side. I walk past two men holding hands to a table in the corner and decide to pull a chair out for Casey. Too much coldness might scare the princess off.

After taking off her thin jacket—more stylish than functional—and hanging it on the back of the chair, she sits down gingerly and seems to seek the position that's best for her beaten ass.

"So what's good here?" she asks.

"Depends what you like," I reply.

She picks up one of the laminated menus from the middle of the table and looks it over. "I'll give anything a try. I don't have any dietary restrictions."

"Then I'd recommend the braised beef noodles in soup. The pasta is hand pulled fresh everyday."

"Sounds good."

A waitress comes over and takes our order. Her curtness seems to surprise Casey. When she leaves, Casey looks around the place skeptically.

"How often do you come here?" she asks.

"Since I have my own chef, not often."

I don't brag, but my being well-off will probably put Casey more at ease. The waitress returns to plunk down our drinks, tea for me and a soda for Casey.

After taking a sip of her drink through her straw, she leans across the table toward me. "So tell me about your fantasies."

"You said you could fulfill them. What do *you* think they are?"

"A threesome. If you're straight, then it's probably two women, one guy."

"And you'd be one of the women for me?"

"I'm okay with two of us going down on you. I'm full on straight, so the lesbian thing wouldn't be my cup of tea."

"You said you'd try anything once."

She pauses to think. "Okay, but she'd better be hot."

"What else?" I ask her. A threesome isn't that creative, and I've done it before.

She takes another sip of her soda. "What are you into? Water sports? Pet play? TPE?"

"All of the above."

She gives me a playful smile. "Me too."

I refrain from shaking my head. She'd agree to TPE with someone she just met? How reckless can she get, or is she faking it to get into my pants?

"What are your fantasies?" I ask.

She perks up. "I've got a lot of different ones."

"Like?"

"Like finding a Dom who can make me squirt."

"Don't just rely on the guy. You've got to do your own homework too."

She gives me another coy smile. "It's more fun doing homework with someone else. Or maybe you can be my taskmaster and punish me if I don't do my assignments."

I only smile in response. She has a relentless streak in her.

"You up for degradation or humiliation?" I ask.

"Yes."

"Gang bang?"

"Yes. Maybe throw in a little consensual non-consent."

I raise my brows.

"You guys can use me and abuse me," she elaborates. "I'll pretend like I don't want it, so you can show me how strong you are by overpowering me."

"You like role-playing?"

"There was a time I thought about becoming an actress. I'd be good at role-playing."

"What about a kidnapping fantasy?"

She purses her lips. "That sounds intriguing. Tell me more."

"I'd take you by force. Make you my sex toy for a couple of days. Keep you naked the whole time, using you for my pleasure whenever I want."

She leans in closer, hanging on my every word.

"Maybe I'll fuck you until you pass out. That is, after I degrade you over and over again."

Her breath is uneven. I half expected to have scared her, which wasn't my intent. The words seemed to come out on their own. But her eyes glimmer with interest.

The waitress arrives to set down Casey's bowl of noodles. It seems to take Casey several seconds to release her mind from the scenario I painted for her.

"Can I get a fork?" Casey asks when the server puts down a pair of chopsticks and a spoon, then sniffs the soup. "Smells good."

Grumbling, the waitress digs into her apron and pulls out a fork before walking away to bark at a young couple that just entered to seat themselves.

"She's not the most friendly waitress," Casey says.

"This place is your standard utilitarian Chinese immigrant restaurant. It's about the food. They don't believe in paying extra for ambiance and small talk from your server."

Casey blows on the steaming noodles before taking a bite and then another.

She looks at me in wonder. "This is *soooo* good."

Leaning back in my chair, I watch her eat. She's either really hungry or she really likes her food.

"You want some?" she asks.

Watching her eat, I start to develop an appetite, but I shake my head.

"You sure?"

"I'm sure."

"I've got to get my friends to try this place. These are the best noodles I've ever had, and I've had the linguine at Il Buongustaio," she says, referring to one of the trendy new restaurants in Nob Hill with dishes that cost seven times as much as her current bowl of noodles.

"Didn't the Chinese invent noodles?" Casey asks in between mouthfuls.

"The earliest references and archaeological findings point to China," I say, wondering if she always has such a robust appetite. It's hard to imagine given her slender frame.

"I should order a bowl to go," she says.

I bring the conversation back around to previous topics. "How did you find out about Club de Sade? They have a big BDSM scene in Boston?"

"I've been interested in BDSM for a while now, so when we moved out here to Frisco—I mean San Francisco—our neighbors said people here don't use that term—I googled BDSM club, and it came up first."

"You been anywhere else?"

"I've been to The Lair but I like Club de Sade. Fewer rules. More intimate space. What made you come to Club de Sade?"

You. But of course I respond differently. "Change of scenery."

"Where do you usually go?"

"The Lotus."

"Hm. Don't think I know it."

"It's invitation only."

She looks intrigued. "Really? How come?"

"It's how the owner wants it."

Having finished the noodles, she picks up the spoon to scoop the broth, which is time consuming.

"You can drink it straight from the bowl," I tell her.

"I'm good with the spoon," she responds.

"Fancy table manners aren't required here."

She looks around but doesn't see anyone else lifting their bowls, though a couple of the college students are holding their bowls while they slurp and shovel their noodles. "I'm okay."

I stare at her. "Do it."

"Do...what?"

"Put your spoon down and drink from the bowl."

"I don't need to finish—"

I raise a brow. She understands my expression.

"Yes, Sir."

Setting down the spoon, she lifts the bowl to her mouth and takes a good gulp.

"Finish it," I order her when she puts the bowl down.

Without protest, she does what I tell her. The waitress comes by to refill my tea.

"You finish fast," she remarks to Casey of the now empty bowl.

"It was delicious. Can I get one to go?" Casey inquires.

The waitress nods and leaves. We hear her shouting the order to the kitchen.

Casey turns to me. "So, were you serious about that kidnapping stuff?"

"Why, you interested?"

She tucks a tendril of hair behind her ear. "Maybe."

"You want to be kidnapped?"

"Sounds like it could be fun."

I study her. It could be fun, like she said. Certainly more fun than kidnapping her father, but Liam keeps four bodyguards with him at all times. If this were the streets of Juarez or Kuala Lumpur, I might have considered it more seriously, but getting the jump on four guys without attracting attention is harder to pull off in the US. Jake Callaghan only has two bodyguards but is in Ireland right now. The wife and Casey only have one each.

And Casey *wants* me to kidnap her. So why not?

Chapter 12

Kai

"**I** *KNOW* IT COULD be fun," Casey says when I don't respond. "You ever done it before?"

"No."

"So here's your chance to try something new."

I stall. "I don't know. We just met. Are you even actually twenty-one?"

"I am! I can show you my driver's license."

"Which can be faked."

She furrows her brow and tries to come up with a response.

"Frankly," I continue. "I'm not convinced you're the right sub for me. You talk a good game—"

"Wasn't I a good sub for you tonight? I know I wasn't perfect, but I can be better."

"I'm not in the market for training a sub."

She pouts. "Why not?"

"You're too...virginal."

"Isn't that a turn-on?" she asks in a conspiratorial tone. "You'd be the first one to do certain things to me. Like, if you're into electroplay, you could be the one to pop my electroplay cherry."

"Popping cherries doesn't score points with me."

"Why not? I read stories that men will pay big bucks to do it with virgins."

"Men like that are insecure: they don't have what it takes to satisfy a more experienced woman."

"So if I'm not the right sub for you, who is?"

"Look, princess—"

"The name's Casey. And I'm not a 'princess' just because my family's well-off."

I raise a skeptical eyebrow. "What proves you're *not* a princess?"

She frowns. "Well, I..."

"Ever go hungry? Ever take public transportation? Sleep in bed linen that has a thread count of less than eight hundred?"

She pouts. "Just because I can afford the finer things—what about you? You drive a Ferrari, wear a Valentino jacket, and that ring with black diamonds looks like it costs a lot."

We both look at the ring on my right hand.

"Aren't *you* a princess?" she accuses.

She's not wrong. I'm sure my assets are several times what Liam Callaghan is worth. But I didn't always have a life of luxury.

"I know what it's like to be hungry," I tell her. "I've gone through garbage to get my dinner and slept on a mattress that didn't have any sheets at all."

Her jaw drops. "Really?"

"It was a long time ago. I was lucky enough to be adopted by a couple with means. They changed my life."

She's silent for a beat before saying, "Okay, you can call me a princess."

"As your Dom, I can call you whatever I want."

The words slip out of my mouth, and, catching them, she perks up.

"Yes, Sir," she says.

I sigh. "The spanking you got tonight, that's a small fraction of what I'm capable of. I don't do BDSM lite."

"Great. 'Cause I don't want to do lite either."

"You sure you're up for the hardcore stuff?"

"Yes."

Though I hadn't set out to kidnap Casey and make her my sub—I want to keep my options open—I feel like that's where I'm headed. My conscience compels me to say to her, "You'd be in over your head with me."

"You don't know that."

"And the thing about young people is you don't know what you don't know. And that can be dangerous."

"'Young people'? You make it sound like you're some old fart."

"I'm almost ten years older than you."

"Oh. You are an old fart then."

Her response has me taken aback. No one has ever referred to me as an "old" anything.

She breaks into a wide smile, surprising me with how attractive she can look.

"Is it weird that I want to be your sub even more?" she asks.

"No, because you have daddy issues."

She sits back and exhales loudly. "Christ, you're..."

The waitress returns with the bill and Casey's order in a plastic bag. Taking out my wallet, I set down a Ben Franklin, even though Casey is the one who originally asked to buy me a drink.

"Time to get you home, princess," I declare. "Or your real daddy might get worried."

She seems to reach the same conclusion and gets up quickly. She puts on her coat, I put on my jacket, and we head outside.

"You want me to drop you off back at the club or do you want to take your car?" I ask.

At her puzzled look, I glance toward where her car is parked.

She blushes. "That, um, that's..."

"A perk of being a princess: you have your own personal chauffer."

"Right. My chauffer. So about being your sub—"

"I didn't say you were my sub."

"You referred to yourself as my Dom."

Before I could answer, we hear items falling. I walk to the end of the building to an alley and see a cat with its paw stuck in some metal twine. It tries desperately to yank itself free.

Casey gasps. "Poor thing!"

I walk over, scaring the cat, but it has nowhere to go.

"Take it easy," I tell it. "I'll get you out."

Based on its scraggly, malnourished appearance, it's a stray and was probably doing some dumpster diving for food. Wrapping a hand around the cat to hold it in place, I unwind the twine from its paw. As soon as the cat is free, it darts away.

"I'll walk you to your car," I tell her.

"You think the kitty will be okay?" she asks.

"Don't know. I'll see if it comes back."

"What do you mean?"

"I'll get some chicken from the restaurant and set it out for the cat."

"What if rats get to it first?" she asks with a grimace and looks around as if the mere mention of rodents might attract them.

"I was going to stick around for a while."

She seems surprised. I don't blame her. Hanging out in an alley in the middle of a winter night is not something most people plan on doing. But strays are my thing because I was one once.

"I'll keep you company," she says.

"Doesn't princess need her beauty sleep?"

She narrows her eyes at me. "You think I'm some spoiled, pampered girl who only cares about her looks?"

I give her a look that confirms what she just said. "You mean you're not someone who spends her days shopping, indulging herself with spas, or jetting off on nice vacations?"

Her silence indicates I've hit the nail on the head.

"I'm a college student," she finally replies. "I go to class."

"For what purpose?"

"To get a college degree."

"To do what?"

Again, she's not able to respond right away. I leave it at that and head back to the restaurant to get the chicken.

"I'm only twenty-one. I don't need to have my life figured out yet," she says.

At twenty-one, I was helping my adoptive father move millions of dollars in arm sales.

I tell the server, who greets us more warmly after having received my tip, what I want. She doesn't ask why I want partially cooked chicken on a plate and heads straightway to the kitchen.

"Did you know what you wanted to do with your life at twenty-one?" Casey challenges me.

"Yes," I reply. "Follow in my father's footsteps."

"Well, I have no interest in following in my father's footsteps. And even if I did, I don't think my father would allow it. He just wants me to get married."

"Already?"

"Yes! He even has the guy picked out."

Intrigued, I ask, "Who?"

"A 'good' Irish boy," she answers, rolling her eyes. "I mean, this is the twenty-first century for fuck's sake."

"Who's the lucky guy?"

"Kenton Brady. He went to Notre Dame, and his family's—" She catches herself and seems to select her next words carefully. "His family's in the same line of business as my dad."

Kenton Brady's name is already in my dossier on Casey because his family is also Irish mafia, but I make a mental note to find out more about him.

"Does your dad want a marriage or a merger?" I ask. "Or are they one in the same?"

"They're the same for him!"

"So princess doesn't want to do what daddy wants?"

"Hell, no. I've already done a lot of what he's wanted. I went to Notre Dame because of him. I would have preferred to go to UC Merced. Closer to Mammoth Mountain."

Even though I had told her this wasn't a date, I end up asking date-like questions. I tell myself that the more I know her, the better my position will be.

"You like to ski or snowboard?"

Her eyes gleam. "Snowboard. I *love* it. I've done a few snowboard cross events, and it's amazing."

"You like speed."

"It's fucking exciting."

Between the BDSM and snowboarding, I wonder if she's an adrenaline junkie.

I take the chicken from the server and head back to the alley.

"You a cat person?" Casey asks me.

"No. I own a dog."

"What kind?"

"She has some German Shepherd. Not sure about the rest. She was a stray I picked up."

"Awww, how nice of you."

"No tag, no microchip," I say as I recall how easily Athena took to me, like she knew she was being rescued.

After setting down the chicken, I lean against the wall and wait.

Casey leans against the wall next to me. "When I was a girl, I wanted a kitten soooo bad. But my father doesn't like animals, so we never got one."

"You're an adult now."

"They don't allow pets in the dorms, but I think I might try off-campus housing next year. Then I can get a cat. If my parents let me go off campus. My dad thinks the dorms are safer."

"Why is safety such a big concern for him? Plenty of college students live off campus."

"He's just...paranoid."

"You always do what your parents want you to do?"

"Well, I'm not marrying Kenton."

"Yeah?"

She hesitates. "My dad has a...stressful job, I guess, and a unique one. And my mom has bouts of anxiety. Sometimes the smallest thing my brother or I did would send her into an episode. So I try not to upset them."

"I'm gonna guess they don't know about Club de Sade?"

Her eyes widen. "Hell, no!"

"Is that your way of secretly rebelling against your parents?"

"Maybe. BDSM is my outlet. And I genuinely love it. So how 'bout it?"

"How about what?" I return even though I know what she's asking.

"You and me. We'd make a good Dom and sub."

"How do you know?"

She rubs her arms against the cold. It's colder than usual for San Francisco. I would have thought someone from the Midwest could handle the cold, but Casey isn't dressed for any kind of winter.

"I just do," she replies.

I pull her into me to warm her up.

"You think so too," she adds, snuggling into my side, "or you wouldn't have agreed to go out with me."

"I wanted to explore the *potential*," I correct her.

"And?"

"I haven't decided."

"What else do you need to know to make your decision?"

She's still shivering, and I think to call it a night. But then I see the cat poke its head around the recycling bin.

"Don't move," I say quietly to Casey.

She sees it too. The cat looks at the chicken, then us, then the chicken. It takes a step forward, then retreats. We watch it as it takes several tentative motions toward the chicken. Halfway between the chicken and the recycling bin, it stops, ready to rush back to relative safety. When it feels more confident, it advances to the chicken. I tighten my embrace on Casey.

The cat makes it to the chicken, grabs it, and runs off.

"You look like you're going to end up with hypothermia if we stay out here much longer," I say and start walking her out of the alley.

"Look, I'm not asking for a long-term commitment," she says. "What's the harm in us playing one more time? If you like it, we can do some more. If not, we move on. It's not like either one of us will have a hard time finding another partner."

I pretend to give it a moment's thought before answering, "Okay. Tomorrow night. Club de Sade at ten o'clock."

The truth is, I wouldn't mind playing with her again.

"Awesome," she replies.

I nod toward her car and 'chauffer.' "You should get home in case your parents start to worry."

She smiles. "Club de Sade at ten!"

I watch her hurry across the street to her car. Once she leaves, I get into my car and call Andrian. It's midday in Moscow.

"*Nakonets*!" Andrian answers. "You have an update, yes?"

"More than that," I reply. "I have a plan."

Chapter 13

Casey

I'M OVER THE MOON. I can't remember feeling so excited about a guy before. Not since I was a tweener and got to meet my favorite boy band after their concert. The non-date couldn't have gone better. Even though I was starting to freeze my ass off in that alley, I got to have his arm around me. I wasn't expecting it to feel so good because I'm mostly interested in his BDSM skills, but his embrace had felt warm and protective.

"Got you some noodles," I tell Chase as I open the car door. "I'll drive."

Chase accepts the takeout bag and gets out to let me drive. After wincing when I sit down, I crank up the heat and start driving.

"Sorry if the soup's cold."

Chase slides the chopsticks from their wrapper and digs in. "Still tasty."

"You know how to use chopsticks?" I ask.

"I grew up here. You go to enough Asian restaurants, you pick it up."

"They have forks."

"Wuss."

"Can you eat any louder?" I ask after he shovels large mouthfuls of noodle.

"I'm hungry. So who's this guy anyway?"

"Said his name was Jack."

"Jack what?"

"I don't know. Why do I need his last name? I'm not dating him."

"You don't want to look him up on the internet? He seems loaded. Bet that would make your parents happy."

"My dad's set on Kenton," I remind Chase.

"So if you and Jack aren't dating, does that mean you're not seeing him again?"

I smile broadly. "Actually, I'm meeting him tomorrow night."

"Lucky you."

"I know, right?"

I beam the whole ride home. When I make it home, I encounter my dad in the hallway. He's dressed in a suit.

"Why are you back so late?" he demands.

"I was hanging out with Aleisha," I reply. It's the truth. I was with Aleisha, just not the whole time.

"Aleisha. Who's Aleisha?"

I can tell he's not keen on the sound of the name.

"A girl I met when we first moved out here. She's really cool. You should meet her."

"I'm busy," my dad replies. "In fact, I've got to hop on a call with someone in Saudi Arabia."

No wonder he's in a suit at this hour of the night. I yawn, wish him good night, and head to my room.

After changing out of my clothes, I lie in bed thinking about Jack. The hours are going to pass by so slowly. I'm too excited at first to sleep, so I text Aleisha that Jack agreed to play with me again. I don't get a response because Aleisha might be asleep. I hug myself. There's something about Jack that's so magnetic, apart from how he can inflict such delicious pain to my backside. I'm used to brash, cocky men. Jack is so...quiet. But he's no less confident. Maybe even more so because he doesn't feel the need to show off.

I think about my still burning ass and wonder what he has planned for me tomorrow. He had said something during our play that he already expected me to blow him, or something to that effect. But I never got to touch him. He didn't even take off his shirt, like he hadn't broken a sweat. What does he look like without clothes?

I recall the orgasm I had. I want another. Like, right now. Getting out of my bed, I dig through my dresser drawer for my vibrator. I replay the scene with Jack. It was definitely my favorite birthday gift.

My climax with the vibrator takes the edge off my need, but it's nothing compared to my orgasm with Jack. At least I feel more relaxed now. I drift off to sleep wondering what Jack will do with me tomorrow night.

*****

"A group of us, including Kenton, are going to go out for drinks tonight," Hannah tells me as we sit in the sauna of the fitness club we use.

"I'll pass, thanks," I reply, adjusting the towel around me.

Hannah, reclining on a wooden chair, sits up and looks at me. "You have other plans?"

"Maybe."

Intrigued, she leans toward me. "Like what?"

I try not to smile too broadly. "I met someone."

She furrows her brow. "A guy?"

I lean back against the wall without answering.

"Who?" Hannah presses.

"Jack."

"Not Jack O'Bryan?"

"He's definitely not an O'Anything."

"Then who is this guy?"

"I doubt you'd know him."

Maybe I shouldn't have told Hannah my plans. What if she mentions it to her mom, who mentions it to mine, and then it gets to my dad? Shit.

"Look, don't tell anyone," I add. "Everyone's so fixated on me getting together with Kenton."

"Well, yeah, you two make such a hot couple."

"Kenton's not that interested in me."

"Yes, he is. He got you that beautiful emerald bracelet for your birthday."

I think about what Jack gave me for my birthday. I'd take that over an emerald bracelet any day.

"I'm not that interested in Kenton."

Hannah looks at me like I'm crazy. "Did you hit your head? Maybe you took a bad fall while snowboarding once? Maybe you need glasses? Have you seen what Kenton looks like?"

I sigh. Hannah doesn't get it.

"He's just not my type, I guess," I say, hoping that will end the conversation.

"So is this Jack of yours hotter and wealthier than Kenton?"

"Actually, he is. And on top of that, he's sweet."

She does a double take. "Sweet?"

"Yeah. We came across a stray, he helped it get untangled from some trash and went to get food for it. We then waited in the alley to see if it would come back."

Hannah wrinkles her nose. "The guy made you stand in a trash filled alley for a cat?"

"He didn't *make* me," I retort, thinking he could have made me do just about anything—I was that thirsty for him. "I wanted to. Kenton would never have done anything like that."

"How do you know?"

"When he was at Notre Dame living off campus, he told me how he and his housemates had a BB gun, and they had this ongoing competition with who could kill the most animals with it. Birds and squirrels were like a point each. He won because he shot a gopher."

"Your parents aren't going to be happy you're seeing some other guy."

"I know, so please, please don't say anything. I mean, I just met the guy. In less than two weeks, I'll be back at school. So this is like a winter break fling. No big deal."

"What are you and this Jack doing tonight?"

"Clubbing."

"So what do I tell Kenton if you don't come to drinks with us?"

"Just tell him I'm not up to it. It's not his business anyway if I have other plans."

"Did you sleep with this Jack guy?"

"On the first date?"

"What? It happens all the time at school."

"No, we didn't sleep together," I reply, silently adding, *Not in the traditional sense. But if I'm lucky, I'll make it past 'first base' tonight...*

I spend the afternoon with Hannah. Back at home, I rewatch video clips of some of my favorite snowboarders like Chloe Kim and Lindsey Jacobellis. Hannah continues to text me trying to get me to join her and Kenton later. My mom, preferring warmer weather, decides she's going to visit her sister down in Palm Springs. She's barely gone two hours before a woman who looks just a few years older than me shows up at our house. The woman wears a skin-tight dress that makes no sense for casually stopping by someone's house.

From upstairs, I glimpse her as she heads down the hallway toward my father's office. Seriously? He can't get a hotel?

Deciding I'm going to tell my dad just that, I stomp my way downstairs, but Maria, one of our house staff, accosts me.

"Mr. Kenton Brady is here to see you," she informs me.

"What's up?" I greet, not particularly excited for him to show up unannounced.

"I wanted to see that you're okay," he replies. "Is there somewhere we can talk?"

I lead him into the living room.

He looks around. "Someplace more private?"

"You didn't want to just call?"

"You see, that's what I'm talking about."

I'm taken aback. He just got here and has barely said anything to me. What is *he* talking about?

"I get the feeling you're blowing me off," he says.

"If I was blowing you off, I'd be ghosting you, not responding to your texts."

"Hannah says you're not going out with us tonight."

"Yeah. Trying to save my energy to do some snow-boarding."

That probably didn't sound all that believable, but I'm not sure I care that much.

Kenton narrows his eyes at me. "What's your deal?"

His tone ruffles my feathers. "What do you mean by that?"

"You dating some guy your father doesn't know about?"

"Last I heard, you are with Courtney," I deflect.

"I broke it off with her for you."

"I didn't ask you to do that. You're not seriously going to go through with what our fathers want?"

He looks at me like I'm the crazy one. "This is important, Casey."

"It's more *crazy* than anything," I correct. "If my dad wants to partner with your dad, they don't need us to do that."

"They probably don't trust each other enough, so our marriage would be the glue that holds this partnership together."

"That's bullshit. Just because we suddenly become family, doesn't mean people can't or won't stab each other in the back."

"Look, the Bradys have been mafia for generations. The Callahans too. It makes sense to look for new opportunities out here in California together."

"Then work with my brother. I don't really care about the family business."

"You can't not care, Casey."

"I didn't ask to be born into this particular family."

"What's so bad about being born a Callahan? You've got everything you want. You'd rather be born to some crack whore in the projects or something?"

This conversation is going nowhere, and I want to bring it to a close.

As if he senses the end of my patience, he changes his demeanor. "Look, I know you probably think I'm not the settle down and get married type, but I've had my fun, and I'm willing to take the whole family thing seriously."

"Well, I'm not. I haven't even graduated college yet. I'm not ready to settle down."

"What do you even need to graduate college for?"

I shrug. "I don't *not* want to graduate from college."

"You can go to college *and* get married."

"I just don't feel like marrying yet."

He shakes his head. "What more do you want from me?"

"I didn't say it was about you. I said I just don't feel like getting married anytime soon."

He runs a hand through his hair and starts pacing. He stops. "Getting married isn't gonna stop you from doing any of the things you want to do."

Ready for him to leave, I say, "Fine, I'll think about it. Just give me some space to wrap my head around it."

It's probably not the answer he wanted to hear, but he grudgingly accepts it. "Sure you don't want to come out with us tonight?"

I nod.

He shakes his head as he leaves. With Kenton gone, I go upstairs to my room to plan my outfit for the night. I want to look my sexiest because Jack is the Dom of my dreams. Aleisha might tell me I'm rushing to judgment, but I feel it deep in my belly. It even feels momentous. Like my life won't ever be the same.

Chapter 14

Kai

ANDRIAN LIKES MY PLAN, though he still talks about ripping Liam a new one, but he agrees logistically it will be harder to get the jump on Liam. The daughter is practically a bird in hand, I explain.

"I won't be back from Moscow for at least three days," Andrian laments.

"I'll handle it," I reply while driving back home after my time with Casey.

"Who's going to do it? Your man Andy?"

"Andy will help, but I'm going to oversee the job myself."

"*Khorosho*. Andy is good, but this, it is too important."

"My thoughts exactly."

"So when will you kidnap this little bitch?"

"Soon."

"How soon? My guys are hearing rumors Liam plans to hold auction in less than two weeks."

"*Imet' terpeniye*," I tell Andrian. "I've got it under control. Trust me."

"Of course, of course. Keep me updated."

Once I'm back at home, I replay the night's events in my head, remembering how nicely her ass glowed red for me, how she ground herself unabashedly on the handle of the flogger. Wondering how many times I can make her come, I start to feel warm. I unbuckle my belt and undo my pants to reach for my cock. Casey's a cute plaything. To my surprise, I didn't have to hold back too much with her. Still, she's out of her depth with me.

Her sticking around with me in the alley surprised me too. It didn't smell great back there, and it was cold. Not a place I expected someone with her background would want to be in the middle of the night. But she didn't complain.

I jerk myself off before getting ready for bed. The following morning, I talk through my plan with Andy and how the logistics would work out. Andy used to work kidnappings before coming to me. His biggest job, kidnapping a Hong Kong tycoon as he left his own residence, netted sixty million US dollars for the *Jing San.*

I have a guy on Casey, and he reports that she went to a gym, hung out at a café with her cousin where they spent half the time chatting and half the time independently on their phones, and spends the rest of the time at home until it's time to meet me at Club de Sade. He tells me that she left the house in her car with her bodyguard.

Dressed in jeans and a casual button-up shirt over a tee, I choose to drive my more inconspicuous Audi. My men follow me in two separate cars.

We arrive at the club early. I wait for Casey outside in my car. I don't plan to play at Club de Sade tonight. Not enough privacy. Plus, I want to impress Casey with a superior club, The Lotus.

When I see her, I get out of my car and intercept her before she heads inside. I notice she has on a thicker coat tonight.

Seeing me, her eyes light up. "Hey."

"We're going to someplace better tonight," I tell her.

"Yeah? Where?"

"The Lotus."

"You said that place was by invitation only."

"I got you an invitation."

It hadn't been easy convincing Darren to allow the daughter of a mafia member into The Lotus. Darren was in a bad mood. Has been for several months. Darren has big shoes to fill in the triad, and maybe the stress is getting to him. But I've also heard it might have something to do with a woman he was seeing. A guy from his security detail had told one of mine that Darren had even taken a bullet for her. That's serious shit.

The only people I would ever take a bullet for are my adoptive parents, but they've both passed away. While the triad is my extended family, I've been a loner most of my life. Andrian would probably be the closest thing to kin.

"Cool," Casey says. "Let me just tell my b—chauffer. Where's The Lotus?"

"I'll drive. Your 'chauffer' can follow us."

Casey goes to talk to her bodyguard. When she comes back, I walk her to my car.

"This is different," she remarks of the vehicle.

"I don't always feel like showing off," I reply as I take her bag. "You've got everything? Your phone in here?"

"Yeah, everything's in there."

I place the bag in my trunk, which has a device that interrupts cellphone reception so her bodyguard can't track her by phone.

"So is that guy really your chauffer?" I ask when we're buckled in our seats. I gaze at her, letting her know that I know.

"No, he's not," she relents. "He's actually a...body-guard."

I don't say anything as I pull the car from the curb and glance in the rearview mirror to see that Chase has pulled into the road too.

"But don't worry," Casey adds quickly, "he won't get in the way."

"Why do you have a bodyguard?" I inquire.

"Dad says most wealthy people do."

"How does he define wealthy? There are plenty of millionaires who don't have bodyguards. Is your dad a billionaire?"

"No, but I guess he makes enough that—I mean, I think it's ridiculous. I don't need a bodyguard, but my dad's super paranoid or something."

"Does your bodyguard follow you everywhere?"

"Well, not into the bathroom, but pretty much everywhere. It sucks."

"He keep tabs on you in other ways?"

"Other ways?"

"Tracking devices, maybe?"

"No. I am *not* wearing a tracking device."

"And he doesn't tell your parents about your extracurricular activities?"

"I've got the goods on Chase. My dad would flip out if he knew that Chase was gay."

In the rearview mirror, I see one of my guys pull his car in front of Chase's. Chase gestures and tries to change lanes, but my other guy is driving next to Chase, blocking him. I turn onto a street that's only one lane each way and start to create more distance between me and Chase, who can't get past my driver.

"My dad was like that," I say.

"I'm surprised my dad was willing to move out here to San Francisco, but I'm glad he did. I like it here. So this place we're going to, The Lotus, why is it so exclusive?"

"Quality control, and the club owner likes to know his patrons."

"How'd you score me an invitation?"

Darren trusts me not to be careless. It isn't enough that I'm *Jing San*. He learned the hard way on that one.

"The guy owed me a favor," I answer.

"Nice of you to have used it on me."

"So don't disappoint."

"Don't worry. I won't."

"What's in the bag you brought?"

She grins. "An outfit."

"What kind of outfit?"

"You'll see."

Chase is no longer visible in my rearview mirror. It's not a far drive to The Lotus, which is in a building of black glass four stories tall. There's no signage to indicate what's inside. I pull up in front, and two parking valets open our doors for us.

"They don't allow cellphones in the club," I explain to Casey after I grab her bag and we head inside. "It's to protect patron privacy."

The club has reception interference, but everyone is required to leave their phones at the coat-check and walk through a metal detector. I can tell Casey is impressed with the lobby with its marble flooring and golden wall sconces with hand-sewn silk shades.

"Why so many bouncers?" she asks of the security guards as one of them double-checks to make sure we're on the guest list.

"People have tried to crash the club before," I reply.

"Can I tell my friends that I got to come here?"

"Sure."

The front of the club is a typical club with a bar, lounging area, and dance floor. The back of the club is where the BDSM action is.

"Go through the women's restroom. You can change in there if you want, then go through the entry in the back," I explain to Casey. "I'll meet you on the other side."

Walking through the men's room, I enter the part of the club reserved for BDSM members. Unlike Club de Sade, The Lotus mostly has private rooms. There are a few open rooms without a fourth wall and a stage for exhibitionism. Right now, there are three women utilizing the stage. One of them, on her hands and knees, is penetrated from behind while she performs cunnilingus on another woman.

After a few minutes, Casey emerges and comes to stand next to me. "That kind of stuff turn you on?"

"Why not?" I respond.

"I think it's interesting how straight men will get turned on by lesbian action, but I don't think straight women feel the same way about gay men. At least I don't."

"Maybe you just need to give it time."

She seems to consider it. A staff member walks over to us to see if we need anything, such as a rapid STD test kit.

"What service," Casey says after I accept two of the kits.

"Follow me," I direct her. "I've got a room reserved for us."

I walk her up to the second level and, opening the second door to our right, we enter a room with dark wooden floors and walls. It's relatively sparse, but I like it because it has plenty of beams overhead to facilitate bondage suspension. I drop my bag onto a table, and we each take a test kit.

While we wait for the results, I say, "Let's see this outfit."

Teasingly, she undoes the buttons of her coat. It falls to the ground revealing her fishnet bustier with an open bust design. The bodysuit comes down to her hips and ends in garters attached to thigh-high stockings. A black G-string covers her mound.

"Turn around," I command.

She does, showing me her ass, which has some bruising from where the cane struck her last night.

"Nice," I compliment.

"I'm glad Master likes it," she says with an impish sparkle in her eyes.

I walk up to her to get a closer look. Cupping a breast, I run my thumb over her nipple. She gasps softly. I rub my thumb around the nipple until it peaks. Slowly, I tug the hardened knob until she grunts.

Stepping back towards my bag, I say, "I have an accessory that'll go well with your outfit."

She seems intrigued. "Yeah?"

From my bag, I pull out a black leather hood. "You ever wear one before?"

"No, Sir. I've done blindfolds before but not a full hood."

"You claustrophobic?"

"I don't think so."

"We'll find out in either case."

I walk over to her with the hood. Her breath goes uneven with excitement. I place the hood over her head. It has a corset style closure from the top of the head to the back of the neck.

"How's it feel?" I ask as I pull on the laces to make the hood fit more snugly.

"I like it, Sir."

Aside from two holes for the nostrils and an opening for the mouth, the hood covers her whole head. I buckle the collar around her neck and reach around her front to grab a breast. "You remember your safe word?"

She grumbles," Yeah."

"What is it?"

"Can I have a new safe word?"

"No." I smack her across the breast. "That's for forgetting to say sir."

"I'm sorry, Sir."

"What's your safe word?"

"Maeve, Sir."

I turn her toward the center of the room. "You're going to take about five steps forward."

After she's in place beneath a beam, I go back to my bag and retrieve a cord of rope, which I fold in half.

"How's that ass of yours doing?" I ask as I wrap the rope, leading with the looped end, around her chest above her breasts.

"Good, Sir."

"Is it still sore?"

"Yes, Sir."

"You think it could take more tonight?"

By her pause, I guess that it's not something she wants. But I know she wants to impress me.

"Yes, Sir."

I wrap the rope below her breasts. "You ever had to use your safe word?"

"No, Sir."

"Would you like to tonight?"

Her breath stops. I ask not because I intend to push her hard enough that she'll use her safe word, though it may come to that. Just putting the idea into her head that I might will get her pulse quickening.

"If that's what you want, Sir."

After I finish up the shinju style chest harness, I toss the rope over the beam and let it dangle behind her.

"You're going to stand on one leg and bend the other," I instruct.

She wobbles as she complies. She'll regret wearing such high-heeled shoes.

Using the other end of the rope, I bind her right ankle to her upper thigh. Going back to the bag, I retrieve a shorter cord of rope, which I use to bind her wrists together.

"Like that?" I ask when I'm done.

"Yes, Sir."

"Good. Now comes the fun part."

Chapter 15

Casey

"I'M ALREADY HAVING FUN," I say. And it's true. I love how the rope feels against me. It's just the right amount of tightness. I've always wanted to be with a Dom who is well-versed in rope bondage. I once came across a guy who seemed to have a lot of skills in that department, but he was older and faintly resembled my father, so I took a pass.

The hood is cool too. There's something naughty and titillating about being objectified – when I want to be objectified. When I haven't given permission, that's another story. But, Jack can objectify me all he wants.

"You're a tease, aren't you?" he responds. "A slutty little tease."

I grin.

He slaps me hard across one ass cheek. "You know what I like to do with slutty little teases like you?"

"I'm excited to find out."

He spanks me hard again. "Sir."

"Sir," I add.

"You have any heart conditions or other health issues I should know about?"

"No, Sir."

His hand encircles my throat from behind, and the reality of being in a private room sinks in. It's just me and him. He could do anything he wanted to me, and I wouldn't be able to stop him. The thought is both thrilling and a little scary. But Jack seems like a responsible Dom. He wouldn't have pressed me on the safe word if he was just going to do whatever he wanted.

Plus, I assume that Chase is not too far. Though I didn't actually see him drive up to the club, and he won't be able to get in without an invitation, there's really no need for me to be paranoid. Most women don't have to drag around a bodyguard wherever they go.

Jack reaches his other hand between my legs, caressing my wetness to flow. He notes, "So wet already."

That's 'cause you turn me on like crazy.

But with his hand firmly about my throat, I don't feel like voicing my thoughts out loud.

He rubs my soaking G-string into my pussy, then moves his grip from my throat to my mouth and nose, cutting off my air. The first several seconds don't bother me, but then my body writhes, seeking air. I bump against the hardness of his body. He lowers his hand, and I gulp in air. His other hand continues to fondle me between my thighs, causing my clit to swell.

Before I catch my second breath, he covers my mouth and nose again. I focus on the delicious tingling in my crotch, the warmth spreading from my groin, and last a little longer this time before I start whining and twisting. I try breathing through his hand. My body strains harder.

He releases me. I exhale with relief and draw in a long breath.

"We're going to go longer this time," he tells me.

That was already longer, I want to point out. But I behave. I manage to get in a breath before he cuts off my air again. It's not any easier holding my breath, though. I savor as much of his caresses as I can before my mind has to focus on the more urgent need to breathe. Firmly, he holds me to him, my head pressing against his shoulder. I love feeling him this close to me.

Except I love being able to breathe too, and eventually, I struggle against him. I grunt and buck. What if he miscalculates how long I can last? How the hell am I supposed to say my safe word?

Actually, it doesn't matter. There's no way I'm going to use my safe word this early into our play.

I do my best not to panic, but I don't think I can take much longer. Shit. Let me breathe!

And he does. Loudly, I release the carbon dioxide that had been building and inhale sweet, sweet oxygen.

"Oh my god," I murmur.

"Again," he says.

"How many—?"

But, clamping his hand over me, he cuts off my question. I try to refocus on his fingers stroking my clit through the flimsy fabric of the G-string, which rubs against me, adding to the sensations down there. My concentration doesn't last long because I can't stop wondering how many times he's going to make me go through air deprivation.

My eyes start to water. Standing on one leg, with my wrists bound behind me, I have little leverage. I do push my ass against him, trying to create some separation. I need air.

I try to wriggle free, but he has me crushed against him. He's so much stronger than me. The deprivation of sight seems to make things worse, intensifying how painful it is not to breathe. Pressure spreads through my chest and into my head.

I need air, I need air!

Finally, Jack drops his hand. I get the air that I need and pray that he gives me a break from the breath play.

"Wow," I sigh, leaning against him. I feel a little tired and want to sit down, but I can't. Worse yet, I have to stand on one leg in heels.

"I was worried there," I tell him. "Sir."

"Worried already, princess?"

Pulling aside my G-string, he rubs my flesh. Damn, that feels good. Like crazy good. I groan in delight. I could actually come like this, standing on one leg.

But he withdraws his fingers. I feel them pressing between my lips. Parting them, I take in his digits, tasting myself.

"Taste good?" he asks.

"Yes, Sir," I mumble with his fingers still in my mouth. "Will I get to taste you, Sir?"

"You want my cock?"

"Yes! Sir."

Taking his fingers out, he wipes them on my breast. "You're going to have to earn it, princess."

Bring it on.

I hear him walking away. What is he planning on getting from that bag of his?

Apparently nothing because I hear the door open.

"I'll be back," he says.

"Where are you going, Sir?" I ask.

"Subs don't need to know."

The door closes, and I'm left alone. I hope he just needs a potty break, or maybe he realized he forgot something. But there was a hint of something in his voice. Something sinister? Naughty?

I hope he comes back soon to resume his fondling. His fingers felt so damn good. And that breath play. A little scary but exciting too. Now that I have my breath, I feel so alive, so aware. I want him back now. My pussy aches for his touch.

But he doesn't come back soon. And all I can do is wait. I try to shift my weight around my one poor foot. Damn these heels. My bent leg is starting to feel sore. It's probably fallen asleep.

Come on, Jack. Come back and get me off. Or let me get you off. Most of the guys I've been with usually can't wait to feel the action.

I hate waiting. Not being able to do anything while I wait is bad enough, but he left me *hot and bothered*. That makes it ten times worse.

Where the hell is he? What if he doesn't come back? No, he wouldn't do that. What would be the purpose in that anyway?

I'm going to die of boredom if he doesn't return in the next minute or so.

I'm not sure how much time has passed when the door finally opens. Footsteps enter. I assume it's Jack, but I can't be certain.

"Sir?" I ask.

The door closes. I hear a chair being lifted and set down. I hear Jack—I'm going to assume it's Jack—sit down. He doesn't say anything.

"Sir?" I prompt again.

Silence. Is this some kind of test? What if it's not Jack? But if not him, who? It's not likely that some random patron would wander into this room, right? Then again, I really don't know this place. Did Jack send someone to look in on me? How long is he going to just sit there?

Chapter 16

Kai

FROM WHERE I SIT, I can tell she's regretting the heels she chose to wear. I see small shifts in her weight, but she doesn't have a lot to work with. I once had a sub wear heels so high she couldn't walk without assistance.

Now that I see her whole body, practically nude, stretched before me, there's more to appreciate. She has both tone and substance. The tits are nice-sized, not too small, not too large. And there's a flare to her hips, which I prefer over stick figures. She's had a recent bikini wax based on how smooth her skin is about her G-string, but she left a small patch of pubic hair, which I had felt earlier.

I adjust my crotch.

Any moment now she's going to say something. Patience isn't an attribute of hers. Yet.

"Admiring the view?" she asks.

I get up and walk over to her. Grasping her nipple, I twist it until she cries out.

"Admiring the view, *sir*," I correct.

"I wasn't sure it was you."

"Excuses," I dismiss and twist her other nipple.

"Shit!" she swears.

I release the tormented nub.

"Thank you, Sir," she says.

"Don't thank me yet."

Going over to my bag, I retrieve a chain with nipple clamps, which I apply near the base of her rosy buds. She barely grunts, so I reposition the clamps closer to the tips of her nipples. She whimpers.

I tug on the chain. "Now you can thank me."

She gasps. "Thank you, Sir!"

"Open your mouth."

When she does, I place the chain between her lips. "Hold onto this. Drop it and we replace these clamps with heavier ones."

Complying, she closes her mouth on the chain, which pulls her nipples back and up toward her.

Standing behind her, I reach my hand into her G-string. She moans immediately. Holding her close, I fondle her slowly, making her wetter than before. With my other hand, I grasp her hair, pulling her head back, which in turn pulls on the chain. Her body quivers.

"I want you to come for me like the slut that you are," I tell her as I curl my fingers into her. "Got that?"

"Yes, Sir," she replies through gritted teeth.

While I slide my fingers in and out of her wet, sloshing pussy, I pull on her hair more. She grunts but angles her hips to allow my fingers deeper penetration.

"That feel good?" I ask.

"Mmm-hmm."

I pull her hair till her head goes as far back as it can.

"Yes, Sir," she murmurs through the chain.

Her cunt juices enable my fingers to glide easily, and I imagine my cock inside her, wrapped with her wet heat. Arousal deepens within me at the thought.

To keep her from getting accustomed to the tug on her nipples, I loosen my hold of her hair before yanking again. Her grunts get more high pitched.

And then I feel her pussy spasming around my fingers. I release her hair as she convulses against me and strains against her bonds. The chain falls from her mouth as she cries out. Her body bucks against me before shuddering. I ease my hand from her crotch and place my fingers at her lips. She takes them and sucks on them weakly. I push my digits toward her throat, making her choke. She starts sucking harder.

"Thank you, Sir," she says after I remove my fingers.

I run my thumb along her lower lip, making it glisten with her saliva. "How does your slut cum taste?"

"Delicious, Sir."

Taking the chain, I yank the nipple clamps off. She screams. I untie her leg next and rub her to encourage the circulation to return.

"Ready for more?" I ask.

"Yes, Sir."

I secure the rope before going to retrieve another cord, which I wrap around her left ankle. I throw the rope over the beam and hoist her leg into the air until her body is suspended parallel to the floor at just the right height for fellatio. But first, I get my set of Japanese clover clamps with weights.

"Since you dropped the chain, you get to try these," I tell her as I crouch down to apply one of the clamps.

"Oh, fuck!" she cries when I allow the weight to fall free.

I attach the other clamp. "Fun, aren't they?"

She gasps sharply before saying, "Yes, Sir."

"Want them heavier?"

"No! I mean, no thank you, Sir."

I tap one of the weights to make it swing. She whimpers through gritted teeth.

Standing up, I unbuckle my pants and yank them down along with my boxer-briefs. Taking out my semi-erect cock, I stroke it till it hardens more before pointing it at her mouth.

"Did you check the results of the tests?" she asks.

I had when I returned back to the room, though she wouldn't know that.

"What if I didn't?" I return. "And make you suck me off anyway?"

"Would you do that?"

"Maybe. Maybe not. Either way, you wouldn't know if I was telling the truth."

It seems to sink in that she's in a precarious position, but then she says, "Can I have your cock, Sir?"

"You're trusting me, or do you just not care?"

"I trust you."

Not very smart.

"If you wanted to get away with something, you would've just done it. I'm rolling the dice a little anyway because those tests aren't perfect, so I might as well make the most of the present moment."

She's lucky the test results were negative. She won't be so lucky in other ways.

I place my tip at her mouth. "All right then."

She parts her mouth and takes me, then runs her tongue along the underside. I close my eyes and relish the feel of her mouth around me. I stand still to see what she will do next. She bobs her head up and down my shaft a few times before pausing at the top to swirl her tongue over my knob. I hold my cock in place for her as she teases the flare of the crown with her tongue and laps at it like a ravenous puppy.

I chuckle. "You like your cock, don't you?"

She comes off me to answer, "Yes, Sir. Very much, Sir."

She resumes moving up and down my shaft while gently sucking. Damn, it feels good.

"Princess must have given a lot of blowjobs before," I observe. "That right?"

"I've given my fair share, Sir."

"You like giving head?" I decide to answer my own question. "Of course you do. Because you're a slutty little tease, aren't you?"

"Yes, Sir."

Pulling out, I rub my tip across her mouth. She tries to lick me.

"What about giving head do you like?" I ask.

"I like that it's a little naughty. I like having my mouth used. Sometimes it feels degrading."

"Degrading, huh? Princess doesn't like to be on a pedestal all the time?"

"It's no fun on a pedestal."

"You won't have to worry about me putting you on a pedestal, princess. To me you're just another slut to have fun with."

She sucks me into her mouth, eagerly it seems, and starts blowing me with vigor.

I continue with the dirty talk. "How about it, princess, you like being my dirty little whore?"

"Yes, Sir," she mumbles against my cock.

"Because that's what you are: a dirty little whore. Just three little holes to be used and abused."

She goes down on me harder. I allow myself a moment to relish her warm, wet mouth before pulling out.

"I want to hear you say it," I tell her.

She smiles. "I'm your dirty little whore."

"And?"

"I'm just three holes for you to use and abuse. Your fuck toy to do whatever you please. Use me however you want, Sir. I'm not a princess. I'm your slut."

"You're good at giving head. What if I invited three guys in here and treated them to a free blowjob, would you do it? And before you answer that, know that two of my friends are on the other side of the club. And I'm sure we could find a third to join us. Maybe we go into the kitchen, pull out a busboy, and make it his lucky day."

She doesn't answer right away, possibly contemplating whether or not I would actually go through with what I described. If I weren't planning to kidnap her, I would. Right now, I don't want to complicate my plans. But she doesn't know that.

I slap her across the face. "Answer me, slut."

"I'm yours to use and abuse, Sir."

Now it's my turn to wonder if *she* would really go through with it.

"If it would please you to see me suck off three other guys, I'll do it, Sir."

"Only the sluttiest of sluts would say something like that."

"Would you make them gangbang me too?"

"Would you like that?"

"It's always been a fantasy of mine."

"But you've done a threesome before."

"It wasn't as exciting as I thought it would be. Maybe because I wasn't the center of attention."

"I can make all your slutty dreams come true, but first you've got to prove yourself."

Chapter 17

Kai

I HOLD MY SCROTUM to her lips. "Suck my balls."

Obeying, she cradles them in her mouth. I groan as she tugs on them.

"Now my cock too," I instruct.

When she opens her mouth, I try to jam my cock as far as I can but she starts to choke.

"Relax," I say before trying again.

She suppresses her gag reflex better this time, but I'm still not deep enough to get my balls in, no matter how high I push them up.

Deciding to work on her deep-throating skills, I drop my balls and have her work on taking as much of my dick as possible.

"Make me come," I command.

She moves up and down my cock. Placing my hand on the back of her head, I make her take more of me. It's not easy giving head in her current position. As her neck gets tired, her head wants to fall forward, but doing so means swallowing more of my cock, causing her to gag.

She pauses in her efforts to take me deep to suck me hard. My cock is as hard as it's ever been. I'm willing to bet she'd like a rough face-fucking. I decide to find out. Holding her head in both hands, I thrust my hips at her. She does a pretty good job keeping pace with me, but she does gag, causing her body to convulse in the ropes.

"Now try sucking my balls again," I say.

This time I successfully stuff them into her mouth and watch as her cheeks swell. She's not able to keep her mouthful for long, but it's progress.

I give her a break and a slap to the face. "You didn't make me come."

"Why don't you shove that nice hard cock of yours in my wet hot pussy?" she replies. "I bet it'll feel just as good in there."

I walk over to her backside and slip a finger between her folds. Her pussy is definitely wet and hot. "You on the pill or do I need to get a condom?"

"I have an IUD, so don't worry, I won't be having your baby."

I hadn't planned on having intercourse with her, but her pussy is awfully tantalizing right now, and her blowjob was pretty effective at getting me turned on.

"What're you waiting for? Fuck me already, Sir," she all but dared.

I spank her hard then pinch and grind her clit between my thumb and forefinger. "Stop trying to top from the bottom. If you want my cock inside you, beg. Bed hard."

"Please, Sir, please fuck me. Your little slut got a taste of cock in her mouth, now her pussy wants a taste too. I need you to fuck me and teach me a lesson."

"What kind of lesson do you need?"

"I need to learn to be a better sub, a better whore for her Master."

"Are you saying you're not a good enough whore?"

"Not yet, that's why I need you to fuck me, to punish me with your cock. Use and abuse me, Sir. Show me you're a Master to your bad little slut."

Her words heat my blood. "Sounds like you need a hard fucking."

"Yes, I do, Sir."

"This could get painful."

"Make it hurt, Sir."

At that, I position myself at her pussy and sink into her. She lets out a sharp gasp, then groans as I slide further into her. She feels good—though I haven't come across pussy that doesn't—and I give my own satisfied groan when her pussy embraces me. Starting her off easy, I roll my hips slowly and thoroughly.

She murmurs, "Mmmmm."

Grabbing her hips, I shove myself a little harder. She softly grunts. I stab deeper. She cries out. I make her cry out several more times, then fall back to a gentle thrusting, the lull before the storm. She moans in pleasure till, without warning, I start pounding into her ruthlessly. She asked for it. I'm delivering.

There's nothing but cries now as I drill into her like I'm going to fuck her into the next room. In the mirror across from us, I see that she's gritting her teeth. What sounds like a half gasp, half wail escapes through them. Her fingers curl white-knuckled into her palms. Her head jerks about like a ragdoll on a bumpy roller coaster. The nipple clamps swing like crazy.

I slow down. "That hard enough for you, princess?"

"Yes, Sir," she murmurs.

I slam into her.

"Shit!" she cries.

I resume my pounding, half expecting her to use her safe word, but all she says is, "shit, shit...shit!" I continue my fast and furious pace until she sounds like she's sobbing.

I pause. "Need your safe word, princess?"

"No, Sir."

Damn. She's tougher than I expected. To reward her, I reach a hand underneath to stroke her clitoris. She purrs. The flexing of her pussy is enough to make me climax, but I withhold myself.

"Can I come, Sir?" she asks.

"Yes," I answer because I want to feel her coming around my cock.

I fondle her till she explodes. The spasming of her pussy threatens to send me over the edge, but I resist the urge.

"Thank you, Sir," she says after she's done jerking and shivering.

I pull out of her and walk over to her head. As soon as I place the tip of my cock at her lips, she sucks me in.

"That's a good princess," I say. "Taste your pussy on my cock."

I allow the tension in my groin to build as she goes down on me. Closing my eyes, I savor the swirl of pleasure in my loins, the heat roiling in my balls, and the wet gliding of her mouth along my shaft. With a loud grunt, I piston my hips to my climax. Without needing me to tell her, she swallows every last drop of my cum, then licks me clean.

"Thank you, Sir. Thank you for your cum."

She licks her lips as if she's just finished a rich dessert.

I shake my head as I zip my pants. "A pain slut and a cum slut."

"The best kind of slut," she returns with a smile.

I could leave the hood on her and walk her out of the club right now. One of my guys put a tracker on her car, so we know where her bodyguard is. He's probably still driving around, trying to figure out where we are. It would be so easy. Plus, she's come, I've come. It's a good note to end on.

Instead, I ask, "You up for more?"

"If you are, Sir, yes."

I release her from the suspension bondage and lead her to a wooden pole. While she stands with her back to it, I retie her wrists behind the pole and bind her neck to it with rope. Next, I wrap the rope around her waist and bring it through her crotch, cleaving her pussy lips, before throwing the end over a beam and attaching a bucket.

"I have three-pound weights," I tell her of the metal plates I hold in my hand, "which I'm going to place in this bucket at the end of your crotch rope."

I place one disk in the bucket. She still has the hood on, so I can't read her reaction. I add a second weight. She starts to breathe more visibly but doesn't seem too distressed until I add two more disks for a total of twelve pounds. Her hips and legs are pulled forward, and she's on her toes past the heels of her shoes. After placing a fifth disk in the bucket, I wait for her to use her safe word. She doesn't.

I put a sixth weight in the bucket.

"Oh, shit..." she mutters through gritted teeth.

"That's eighteen pounds on your pussy," I note, impressed.

There are more weights I can go for, but I retrieve a vibrator instead. Turning it on high, I place it against the rope at her crotch.

"Ahhh!" she cries.

"That feel good?"

"God, yes! I'm going to come."

"Already?"

"Yes, please, Sir, yes."

"Do it."

Her torso pumps up and down, and I see her orgasm undulating through her body, her mouth open in a silent cry before she starts to whine. I keep the vibrator going.

"K-K-K," she stutters.

"You can come again," I say.

"It h-hurts now, S-Sir."

"That's what we're here for."

"P-Please—oh shit!"

Trembles erupt through her as I yank the nipple clamps off her. She screams, her body bucking against the pole and bindings. When I turn off the vibrator, her breath is ragged.

"You came again, didn't you?" I inquire.

She exhales and whispers, "Yes, Sir."

I untie the bucket, then remove all her rope bindings as well as the hood. Checking in on her, I look into her eyes.

She meets my gaze. "I need to sit down."

Sweeping her off her feet, I carry her to a sofa and set her down with her legs over my lap.

She puts her head on my shoulder. "That was...wow."

"How's your pussy doing?" I ask.

"Sore—inside and out."

Without thinking, I stroke her hair. "Not bad for daddy's little princess."

I've put subs through more intense activities, but for some reason, I enjoyed the scene with Casey. I shouldn't, given that she's the daughter of my enemy, a man who stole from me and killed one of my best men.

She reminds me of the cat in the alley. Which is absurd. One lives a harsh life on the streets while the other is a privileged young woman who probably overestimates herself because she hasn't had to suffer.

But I can change that. I can bring some suffering into her world.

Chapter 18

Casey

I CAN'T BELIEVE I made it through all that without using my safe word. I came close to using it two or three times. The rough fucking had brought tears to my eyes. But it was so worth it. He felt so good inside of me. And I *love* it when my clit gets touched at the same time my pussy is full of cock.

That rope crotch business was something else too. After coming that first time, my clit was so sensitive, and even though the rope stood between me and the vibrator, I couldn't take it. It hurt. And yet, through the pain, I managed to come. I amazed myself.

And now this, snuggled up to him, my legs over his lap, feels like the perfect ending to a perfect scene.

I had a sense, when I first laid eyes on him, that he might be the Dom I've been looking for. He did not disappoint. The prospect of what else he can do gives me goosebumps.

"Cold?" he asks, wrapping an arm tighter about me.

"Satisfied," I sigh. "Did I really have eighteen pounds pulling on my pussy?"

"You did."

"Where'd you even get the idea to do something like that?"

"When you've been around BDSM as long as I have, you see a lot of shit. Mostly I take what I've seen and just add my own twist."

Wondering how many subs he's had before, I ask, "You do that weight thing a lot before?"

"A couple times."

"What's the heaviest amount of weights you've used?"

"Thirty."

My jaw drops. "That'll slice a pussy in half!"

"Depends on the pussy and the thickness of the rope."

I become silent in thought, trying to imagine how thirty pounds would feel. What else has he done to his subs? Do I want to find out?

Hell, yes!

Remembering one of the topics we talked about last night, I ask, "You ever done a kidnapping role-play?"

He pauses. "Why, you interested?"

"It sounds like fun, the stuff you said yesterday. Maybe you and two of your friends accost me in a parking lot and throw me into the back of a van. I'll struggle, of course, but you guys tie me up and have your way with me."

He doesn't respond right away, and I think maybe I've gone too far by including additional people in the fantasy, but he was the one who mentioned friends in the first place.

"Would that really turn you on?" he asks.

"Totally."

He's silent once more. Am I coming across too slutty? Do I really want to be gangbanged by people I don't know? Yes and no. Mostly yes.

"As long as no one has STDs," I add. "Maybe it's best everyone wears a condom."

"Then what happens?"

I muse aloud, "Maybe you put me in a cage. I'm your sex pet to use and abuse."

"Do I make you sleep in the cage too?"

"I don't know. Sleeping in a cage won't be comfortable, but it fits with the sex pet scenario."

"Or I could lock you up in a locker or a chest. Take you out when I want to play with you."

"Mmmm, that sounds sexy too. Just no coffins. I've seen that done on TV too many times."

We're just talking, but I'm encouraged. Maybe this means I'll get to play with him again.

"So what do you think?" I prompt, sitting up so I can look into his eyes. "Wanna do it?"

He stares at me long and hard. His silence isn't a great sign.

"Didn't I live up to expectations?" I ask. "Wasn't I a good sub for my Master?"

"Pretty good," he acknowledges. "But I'm not looking for a long-term partner."

"I know. Neither am I. I'm only here for winter break, then I'm gone, back at school. You'll probably never see me again unless you decide to be a regular at Club de Sade."

"You really want me to kidnap you?"

"Just for the night. Unless you want to go longer."

He looks away. "You have no idea what you're asking for."

Why did he say that? Is it because he thinks I'm not up to whatever he can dish out?

I lift my chin. "Try me."

He turns to look back at me, and I almost feel like he's looking at that stray cat from the other night, with a touch of pity.

"I'll think about it," he says.

I know better than to push it too much. I don't want to come on too strong, so I accept his answer.

For now.

Chapter 19

Kai

ONCE CASEY GETS HER cellphone back on our way out, she calls her bodyguard. I can hear him even though he's not on speakerphone.

"Where have you been?" he exclaims. "I've been calling and texting."

"I'm sorry, this club I went to doesn't allow phones," Casey explains as we get into my car. "Besides, I thought you were right behind us."

"I was, but it was like I got boxed out. I've been driving all over San Francisco looking for you."

"Jack's gonna drop me back at Club de Sade. You can meet me there."

"You know if anything happened to you, your dad would have my head on a platter?"

"Nothing did happen, so it's all good."

"Just don't let that happen again."

"Okay, okay. Didn't know you were such a worry-wart."

Hanging up, Casey shakes her head. "It's like I have a fucking nanny—and I'm twenty-one years old!"

"The trials and tribulations of being a princess," I remark with little sympathy.

She glowers at me. I grin.

"I had a great time," she says. "Thanks."

"You're welcome."

We don't talk much on the ride over to Club de Sade, which is good with me. I like that Casey doesn't seem to feel the need to fill the silence with conversation.

Her bodyguard is parked right in front of Club de Sade when we pull up.

"So you'll let me know, right?" she asks. "I can call your phone with mine so you'll have my number."

"You can just tell me what it is," I reply.

She lifts a skeptical brow. "You're just going to memorize it?"

"What's so hard about remembering ten digits?"

"It took me weeks to remember mine. You must be good with numbers."

I am, and I only need her to tell me her number once.

"You sure you've got it?" she asks.

"4-1-5-5-5-5-2-8-9-8," I answer without missing a beat.

She looks impressed. "Okay then."

When I don't say anything more, she opens the car door. "I might go up to Tahoe, so let me know soon."

"Sure."

I can tell she wanted more of an answer.

"Thanks again for the fun times," she says before exiting my car.

I watch her as she gets into her own car and wait for them to drive off first. I sit in my car, feeling oddly unsettled. I could have kidnapped her straight from The Lotus, like I had initially planned. It would have been too easy. Maybe that's why I hesitated. That and the thought of fulfilling her fantasy the way she described intrigued me. I'd love to see the expression on her face when that happens. She doesn't hide her enthusiasm, and it's almost contagious. Even the way she ate her bowl of noodles was interesting to watch.

Remembering the cat behind the noodle restaurant, I decide to drive over and see if the stray is still lurking around. Like the night before, I ask for a plate of lightly cooked minced chicken from the restaurant's kitchen and take it to the alley, but I stop in my tracks when I round the corner.

Standing across from a dumpster stinking of rotting food is Casey.

"What are you doing here?" I ask her.

She looks equally surprised to see me and answers, "I was hungry and thought I'd see if that stray cat is still here."

Glancing down at the chicken I hold, she says with a grin, "That's why you're here too."

I put the chicken down and notice her coat isn't thick enough for hanging out in an alley late at night. "Don't you have thicker coats than this? I thought you're from the Midwest."

"I wasn't planning on being out here for long, but now that I've got company..."

We stand silently in the dark for several minutes. Chances are low that we'll come across the stray again, but I hear the rustle of something moving. Casey and I don't move or make a sound. I see a little head poke out from underneath the dumpster. It retreats, then peeks out again. The cat does this several times before venturing her full body out toward the chicken, taking slow tentative steps, ready to dart back to safety if needed.

Casey and I watch as the cat sniffs, then nibbles at the food. Slowly, I take steps toward the cat. She pauses and stares at me for a while before resuming her eating. Eventually, I'm close enough to scoop her up. To my surprise, she squirms but doesn't put up a fight, as if she recognizes me.

"Awww," Casey whispers as I pet the creature. "Are you going to adopt it or should we take it to a shelter?"

I pick up the plate of chicken and hold it up to the cat so she can finish eating. "Shelter's not open at this hour, so I'll keep her for the night."

"I'd take her, but my dad's allergic to cats."

After the cat's done eating, I take her to my car.

"You already get your noodles?" I ask.

She scratches the cat on its head. "We got it to go. My bodyguard has the order. You still have my number?"

I repeat it to her satisfaction.

"Text or call," she says before walking away, "and let me know what you decide with the kitty."

In my car, I turn on the seat warmer and place the cat in the passenger seat.

Back home, Athena greets me at the door. For a dog off the streets, she has developed an amazing disposition. It wasn't like that at the beginning. She had anxiety and paranoia, but now she's calm and devoted. She sniffs at the cat, which I expected to leap out of my arms to hide beneath the nearest sofa. Instead, she seems curious about Athena. The cat's behavior surprises me, but one of her eyes is half closed and cloudy, which makes me suspect that she's sick. When I'm confident Athena won't jump on it, I gently put the cat down to answer my cell. It's Andrian.

"So you do it?" he asks.

"No," I reply. "I changed my mind."

"What? Why?"

I take a beat before replying, "We should consider all alternatives thoroughly before committing to kidnapping the daughter."

"You said it would be easy."

"I know, but I don't want to rush into things just because they're easy."

"We could go with poisoning his family."

Andrian's boss has an obsession with poisoning, maybe the result of his days with the KGB.

"When are you able to come back?" I ask.

"I don't know. Three, four days maybe. But I don't want to wait."

"You know me: I don't like second chances. I want it done right the first time."

"*Da.* Okay. You let me know what you decide."

After hanging up, I sit down and watch Athena and the cat continuing to check each other out. It was nice of Casey to return to the alley to check on the cat. I didn't expect that from an entitled princess.

I shouldn't have any interest in Callaghan's daughter. For that reason alone, I should consider something other than kidnapping Casey.

I type her number into my phone and text her:

It's a no.

She texts me a frowning emoji and:

Anything I can do to change your mind?

I return a simple "No" and receive from her:

I'll be at Club de Sade tomorrow night if you decide
you want some fun.

I'm surprised she accepted my answer, but I think she knows better than to badger me. She sends another text asking about the cat.

Seeing that Athena and the cat seem to be getting along, I decide I'll keep the cat. She might be good company for Athena.

And maybe I'll name her Maeve.

*****

Continue the story with CAPTURED MAFIA
PRINCESS.

When fantasies go awry, can this princess make it
out alive?